MY BIG GRUMPY ALIEN DRAGON

STARLIGHT MONSTERS
BOOK 4

SKYE MACKINNON

Peryton Press

MY BIG GRUMPY ALIEN DRAGON

SKYE MACKINNON

Cover by Gombar Cover Designs

Published by Peryton Press

PERYTONPRESS.COM

SKYEMACKINNON.COM

CONTENTS

To my very own grumpy dragon

Click – minute (30 Earth minutes are 20 intergalactic clicks)

Cycle – day (one IG day has 27 Earth hours; there are 10 IG days in an IG week)

Intergalactic Authority (IA) – law-enforcing organisation (space police), overseen by the Intergalactic Council

Kalumbu Station – the orbiting space station where the Trials are monitored and run.

Peritan – intergalactic term for a human

Peritus – intergalactic term for planet Earth

Rotation – one year in Intergalactic Standard

Valhyr's Crown – planet of the draquari

HAZEL

Run.

That was the only word that mattered. Not think. Not breathe. Definitely not *calm down, Hazel, everything's fine*. Just – run.

Branches whipped at my skin as I charged through the trees, bare feet slamming into soft earth and jagged stone alike. My thighs burned. My lungs burned. Everything burned except for the creature behind me, which apparently didn't understand the concept of exhaustion.

Something roared. A deep, bone-shaking roar that rattled the forest and sent a flock of squawking, crimson-feathered birds erupting from the canopy. I didn't look back. I'd made that mistake five minutes ago and nearly face-planted into a log the size of a bus.

All I focused on was what was right in front of me. Trees in ridiculous garish colours that made the forest look like it was on fire. If I hadn't been naked, exhausted and busy trying not to die, I might have even enjoyed the scenery.

I clutched my only weapon – a splintered branch I'd sharpened with a rock – so tight my knuckles ached. It wasn't much, but it made me feel slightly less like a nude snack and slightly more like a nude warrior snack. Big difference.

Insects much larger than I wanted them to be kept hitting my face. So far, none of them had stung me, but that must have been dumb luck. I evaded something that looked like a beetle the size of a boulder with skin like lava rock while the thing behind me kept roaring.

I could hear it crashing through underbrush – too fast, too big. I hadn't seen it clearly when it appeared, just a glimpse of obsidian hide, gleaming claws, and way too many teeth. Four legs, maybe six. Perfectly built for rough terrain.

Me? I was built for Netflix marathons on the sofa, craft nights with my cat, and sipping tea in Glasgow's West End cafés while pretending I sat there alone because I liked solitude, not because I didn't have any friends.

The ground rose beneath my feet, sloping towards the jagged ridge I'd been crawling towards all day. Mountains made of diamonds. Sharp, glistening peaks that I hoped had water, caves, and shelter. If I could make it that far, I had a shot.

If.

Another roar. Closer this time.

"Oh, come on!" I screamed over my shoulder. "Don't you have something *else* to chase? Like a squirrel? I swear I taste disgusting!"

A root caught my foot and I tumbled forward, scraping my knees on rough bark and stones. Pain flared. I scrambled back up, branch in hand, and stumbled through a narrow gap between two orange-trunked trees just as the thing lunged behind me.

Its breath hit my back like a furnace. I screamed and dove forward – just in time to fall down a steep slope.

The world turned and twisted. I hit the ground hard and rolled. Dirt in my mouth. Blood in my nose. Something hit my head, hard. For a moment, I felt like I was going to pass out.

But then the slope finally came to an end and I came to a stop. Everything was silent.

No crashing. No snarling. No death.

Just birdsong. Wind. Insects. I closed my eyes and imagined I was back home, relaxing on a bench in Kelvingrove Park. Not in this nightmare that I couldn't wake up from. I still didn't know where I was. I just knew that this was not home, not Scotland, not even Earth.

The only other alternative was that I was in some kind of virtual reality game – but I had stopped believing in that theory when I'd sliced open my arm on a jagged branch as hard as rock.

Maybe this was death. The afterlife. Hell.

I most certainly deserved it.

I didn't move for a long time. Just lay there on my side, panting, staring at a fern with leaves like molten glass.

Eventually, I sat up and spat out a glob of blood.

The slope had brought me down into a narrow, rocky hollow. Cliffs loomed above on one side, trees on the other. I could no longer see the diamond mountains except for a pale sliver above the cliff to my right, showing me the direction I'd have to take once I recovered a little.

The air smelled like ash and moss. My spear-branch was gone, probably snapped during the tumble.

I brushed off dirt and checked my arms. A few scrapes. A shallow cut on my thigh. My chestnut hair – what was left of it – was plastered to my face with sweat.

Before I'd woken up on that metal platform in the middle of a fire-coloured forest, I'd had hair down to my waist. I was proud of it. Very proud. Not many people had hair that long. I put a lot of effort into it.

But now it was gone. Someone had cut it while I'd been asleep. I was left with stubble that barely reached the bottom of my ears. I didn't want to know how horrendous it looked. I didn't want to think about who had done it and why.

I didn't cry. Not now. Not when I'd made it a whole day in this hell. Not when my lungs were still heaving and my heart hadn't exploded from terror.

I was alive. Still anxious, still naked, still scared of...
whatever the hell that thing was. But alive.

The monster must have given up on having me for
dinner. But it was not the first thing that had chased me
today. This forest was teeming with deadly animals
wanting to take a bite of me. Which was why I was
headed to the mountains. I hoped there would be less
predators there. Not that I knew for certain. But it was
as good a direction as any.

I didn't know how long I sat there, staring at the
moss-covered rocks and trying not to fall apart.
Could've been five minutes. Could've been an hour.
Time didn't feel right on this planet. Or wherever the
hell I was.

Eventually, the shaking in my legs stopped enough
for me to stand. My head throbbed from where I'd hit it
– just a dull, rhythmic ache now, like a reminder that
yes, I was still alive. Yay. Congratulations.

I rubbed my arms for warmth. The air was cooler
down here, the sun slipping lower behind the jagged
ridgeline of the mountains. I was still heading towards
them, even if the fall had knocked me off track. And
possibly slightly concussed me. But priorities.

I needed shelter. Water. A weapon. Clothes,
ideally, but that wasn't exactly something I could
crochet together from ferns and bark.

I scanned the hollow. The cliffs above were sheer
and fractured, little shards of crystal glittering between
the rocks. One of them might be a cave. Or a crevice big
enough to crawl into and not die in my sleep.

A dry laugh rose in my throat. Strange how my priorities had adjusted so quickly. Back home, I had so many dreams, so many ambitions. I knew I'd never reach them, but that was part of it. It's much easier to self-deprecate when you never achieve your goals. And I was the queen of self-criticism and self-loathing.

No space for that here. I had to survive.

My therapist would be so impressed.

I found a fallen branch – not as good as my last one, but it would do – and started walking, slower this time. Every muscle in my body screamed in protest, but I'd been through worse. Not exactly chased-by-alien-lion worse, but emotionally worse. Which, to be honest, was most of my twenties.

A rustle to my right made me freeze. I held my breath, eyes scanning the trees.

Nothing.

Just a breeze stirring the golden leaves. A flicker of shadow. A reminder that I wasn't alone out here – and probably never would be.

By the time I spotted a shallow overhang in the cliff wall, the sky had shifted to deep amber. The forest glowed like a burning oil painting. Beautiful. Lethal.

And rising across the sky were two moons. Not one. Two.

Final proof that I was no longer on Earth.

Fuck me.

I was on an alien planet. Or I was hallucinating being on one. Or Hell was a real place and it just happened to have two moons.

I focused on the ground in front of me. If I looked up at those moons again, I might erupt into hysterics.

I squeezed into the hollow underneath the overhang and let out a deep breath. Rocks on either side formed a sort of half-cave that gave me a semblance of shelter. Not exactly a five-star hotel, but it would keep me from being spotted from above. For some reason, animals were scarce in this valley I'd tumbled into. Maybe they were scared of me.

As if.

Using a rock, I chipped at the new branch until I had a crude point. Not as sharp as the first one, but I wasn't about to fight off another monster tonight. If they wanted to eat me while I slept, so be it. I wasn't going to be able to stop them once darkness fell. I didn't have a light or fire. I didn't have anything except my laughable weapon.

I curled into a ball on the bare stone, hugging the makeshift spear like a lifeline. My skin stung from scrapes and bruises. My stomach clenched with hunger. But it was the silence that got me.

No cars. No distant chatter. No buzzing phones or cat meows or streetlights outside my flat.

Just me.

And whatever was out there.

I let my eyes drift shut. I didn't think I'd fall asleep any time soon, but exhaustion caught up with me. Sleep came slow and shallow, full of twisted dreams I wouldn't remember. And just before I lost consciousness, I thought I heard something.

Not a roar. Not a snarl.
A growl.
Low. Deep. Mechanical.
Far away.
But moving closer.

I woke to a sound I didn't recognise.

A hum. High-pitched, mechanical, and way too deliberate to be natural.

I froze, pretending I was still asleep. I slowly opened one eye and stared into the fading darkness of my rocky hideout. Pale light filtered through the trees outside – dawn, maybe. The alien sun rising. Warmth slowly returning to my frozen fingers.

The hum grew louder. Closer.

And then I saw it.

A shape drifted past the entrance of my shelter. Small, hovering, barely the size of a football. Smooth and silver, with a ring of lights pulsing around its middle. No wings. No rotors. Just impossible, silent motion.

In the centre of the lights sat an eye. A black iris surrounded by a ring of silver that turned and widened. A camera. That thing was a drone.

My heart stopped. Just for a second. Then it pounded hard enough to shake my ribs.

I was being watched. It had to know I was here. The overhang gave me some shelter, but I was still exposed.

The drone paused – right outside the hollow. A beam of blue light swept across the cliff face, slow and searching. Like it was scanning. When the blue light reached me, a shiver crossed over my skin. I didn't move, still pretending I was asleep, my eye almost closed behind shaking lashes. I didn't dare to breathe.

What was it doing?

It hovered for a few seconds longer, then turned and drifted away – upward, towards the cliffs, towards the mountain range I still hadn't reached.

I stayed frozen until the hum faded into nothing.

Only then did I let myself sit up, shaking.

That hadn't been human. Not by a long shot. The tech was too smooth, too quiet. Drones needed rotors or some other way to stay up. This had been a sphere flying without rotors or wings. Even Earth's top-end surveillance crap didn't move like that. And there was something about the way it *looked* – like it had made intelligent decisions based on what it had found during its scan.

"What the hell is this place?" I whispered.

My voice cracked. I hadn't said much since I'd woken up on the platform yesterday.

I didn't get an answer. Just the wind through the

trees and the distant cry of something I hoped wasn't hungry.

I crawled out of the hollow and stood, knees stiff, muscles aching. A new day had begun, and I still didn't have food. Water. Clothing. Answers. But now I had something new to think about.

Who was watching me?

Why?

And what would happen when they stopped watching and decided to *intervene*?

I should have got up and started the climb back up the slope that I had tumbled down the day before. I should find water and food. I should do *something*.

But instead, I just sat there, trying to process what had happened. How I'd come to be here.

I hugged my knees to my chest. The air was warming, light spilling over the treetops, but the ache inside me didn't lift. My throat ached. My thoughts hurt even more as I remembered.

The platform had been metal. Cold. Smooth. A perfect circle floating maybe thirty feet above the forest floor. No walls. No railing. No people. Just *me* – naked, disoriented, dumped like garbage onto a disc in the middle of an alien forest.

I'd woken up to the sound of wind and a booming voice I couldn't place.

"Paralysis lifted. The Trials have begun!"

That was it.

No context. No face. Just the voice, and the sudden, stomach-lurching drop as the platform began to descend.

No elevator cables. No engines I could see. Just a slow, quiet fall towards a forest painted in fiery reds, oranges, yellows, as if someone had added the wrong filter to an otherwise pretty picture.

I'd screamed. Not because of the descent, but because I'd finally realised what was missing – my hair. My clothes. My memory of how I'd got there.

All gone.

When I hit the ground – gently, somehow – I ran without looking back. There'd been no other option. Just trees in every direction and the gut-deep certainty that *something* was watching. Hunting. Waiting.

And in the distance, the roar of a predator had told me exactly what kind of world this was. One where I was nothing but prey.

A screeching birdcall snapped me back to the present.

I blinked away the memory and stood, stiff and sore. My mouth felt like it had been stuffed with sandpaper. I needed water. And maybe food. If something edible and non-poisonous existed here. From everything I'd learned about this planet, I wouldn't have been surprised if my food ate me first.

I looked up at the slope and decided I lacked the

energy to climb. I'd look for water in this valley first before attempting to retrace my steps. The forest floor was soft beneath my feet – layers of needle-like leaves in crimson and gold. A little too warm, a little too quiet. But something drew me forward.

I was desperate to see traces of civilisation, of people living here, but I didn't need my archaeology degree to know that I was alone out here. No ruins, no remnants of sentient life, not even something as simple as a stone circle that a more primitive culture would leave behind.

Nothing but nature, beautiful and terrifying.

After maybe twenty minutes of walking along narrow animal trails, I heard it.

Running water.

I broke into a jog, dodging a tree with bark like cracked clay, and skidded to a stop in front of a stream.

It wasn't wide – barely the length of my arm – but the water was clear and fast, tumbling over dark, glassy stones.

Would this water be safe to drink?

I didn't have a choice. Without water, I wouldn't last much longer. And I highly doubted I'd find a stash of bottled water somewhere. No, if I wanted to survive, I had to take the risk.

I dropped to my knees and drank. Cupped my hands, filled them again and again. It was cold. Sharp. Refreshing. Slightly metallic but not foul.

Once my thirst was sated, I splashed some water across my face and arms to wash off the blood and dirt.

I looked at my reflection in the ripples, then turned away quickly.

I didn't recognise the woman staring back.

Nearby, I spotted a cluster of purple-tinged berries growing on a bush with waxy, triangular leaves. I poked one with a stick, waited. No smoke. No sudden explosions. No snakes waiting in the undergrowth.

Eventually, I plucked a berry the size of an apricot and held it to my nose. It smelled sharp and citrusy.

Screw it. Death by poisonous berry was more appealing than death by toothy monster.

I ate one. The flavour of juicy limes and sweetness of mango erupted around my tongue. Delicious. But I forced myself to wait for a few minutes. No nausea. No side effects.

I ate a handful more, then placed as many as I could on a large leaf which I rolled into a satchel. Just in case I didn't pass a bush like this again.

It wasn't much. But it was a start.

I should have felt somewhat relieved after this refreshment, but something was off.

The birdsong around me had quietened.

My skin still crawled with unease. My gut whispered that I should not linger. Not here. Not in this place that suddenly felt too exposed.

I pushed forward, following the stream as it wound through the thinning trees. The canopy opened gradually, letting more sunlight flood the valley floor. The brilliant reds and golds of the forest sparkled like flames above me.

A pile of huge dead branches formed a natural archway. I stepped through it and into a wide clearing. The trees pulled back entirely, leaving a circular patch of open ground, ringed by tall cliffs on one side and fiery trees everywhere else. Strange crystals jutted from the rock walls, glittering like jagged diamonds under the pale sun. For a moment, I just stood there, breathing hard.

I was already thirsty again.

The open sky above felt unnerving after the dense forest. Too wide. Too vulnerable.

I didn't like it.

And then came the sound from somewhere up above.

A low vibration. Different from the drone. Bigger, louder.

My chest tightened. I scanned the cliffs, eyes darting. My fingers gripped my stick-spear, holding it close like it could somehow protect me. I knew I didn't stand a chance if this was a flying monster.

The vibration grew. Louder. Heavier.

A shadow slid across the clearing.

I snapped my head up.

Wings.

Huge, jagged wings that blocked out the sun. A monstrous shape descended fast, slicing through the air like a blade. My legs locked in place, too slow to run, too shocked to scream.

Metal gleamed across massive scales. Claws

extended, sharp and curved. Its eyes glowed like molten gold, locked directly on me.

No time.

No escape.

The claws closed around my body, careful but unrelenting. My world spun as I was lifted off the ground, the air rushing past my ears in a deafening roar. I kicked, punched, thrashed, but it was useless. The claws were like iron cages.

The creature climbed higher, carrying me towards the cliffs and the jagged heights where the trees could no longer hide me.

I screamed. Pointless.

Above me, the great head turned slightly. The golden eyes narrowed. And for one insane moment, I swore I saw hesitation in them. Like it was not entirely sure what it was doing.

Or who I was.

Then it beat its massive wings and carried me higher, into the mountains made of diamonds, towards whatever nightmare waited at the top.

I drop my prey on the cave floor.
It wriggles.
I move to block the entrance. No escape.
Small. Soft. Warm.
Not like others.
Skin pale. Eyes wide.
I am not hungry yet. It is for later.
I have time to watch. And stare.
It smells right.
Familiar. Wrong. Right.
Memory stirs.
Deep. Buried. Old.
It is prey.
She is prey.
But she is not food.
Mine.
I breathe her in. The scent curls inside my chest.
It burns. But not like pain.

Different.
Good.
The metal pulls at my mind. The collar tightens.
The commands scream.
Kill. Obey. Fight.
I have to go. Before the pain grows worse.
She curls against the stone. Far from me.
Small sounds. Weak hands. Tiny stick.
I do not understand her sounds.
Her eyes meet mine.
No scales. No claws. No fangs.
But she does not submit.
Strange.
Brave.
The pain claws deeper. The order comes.
Fly. Hunt. Destroy.
I snarl. The metal tightens.
I stretch my wings.
I must go. No choice.
But I will return.
She is mine.

What the fuck just happened?

I rubbed my arms, sore from the beast's tight grip. My skin was already bruising where those claws wrapped around me. Could have been worse. Should have been worse. I was alive. Somehow.

I glanced around. My breath caught at the sight.

The cave was huge. Bigger than any I had ever seen. Jagged crystal formations jutted from the walls and ceiling, glinting faintly with soft, unnatural light. The air was warmer here, thick with the faint scent of smoke and something sharper. Metallic.

I really hoped it wasn't the smell of blood, of my predecessors who had become the dragon's dinner.

Because that's what it looked like, the beast. A fricking dragon. Not quite as in the stories. It wasn't all flesh and turquoise scales, but there was metal attached to its limbs and wings. Unnatural. Extra scary.

There was no door. Just a wide mouth of stone behind me, where the creature had dropped me before curling its enormous body across the entrance. It had blocked my only way out like it was nothing. Just flesh and metal and wings too big for my brain to process.

But it wasn't making any attempts to eat me. Its huge eyes watched me, curiously, cautiously.

I pulled my knees up to my chest, too weak to stand, and forced myself to breathe. Slow. Controlled.

Don't panic, Hazel.

But I did it anyway.

The beast watched me. Its head tilted, those glowing golden eyes narrowing slightly, studying me. Like I wasn't what it had expected.

Its scales shimmered in the dim light, somewhere between turquoise and aquamarine with a hint of mother of pearl. And again and again, metal fused with flesh. Biomechanical. That was the word, right? My brain kept spinning, barely able to hold onto language. The only solid fact was that I had been abducted by a cyborg dragon.

I let out a shaky breath. "Well. What are you going to do now?"

The creature didn't move. It didn't react. Just watched.

I should have been dead. It could have crushed me the moment it found me in that clearing. Ripped me apart in the air. Burned me alive mid-flight.

But it hadn't.

Why?

I hugged my wooden spear tightly, clinging to the only thing that felt remotely like safety. The berries were gone, dropped at some point mid-flight.

My mouth was dry again, but I didn't dare move towards the thin stream of water trickling along one side of the cave. Every inch of my skin felt exposed under its heavy gaze.

"Are you going to eat me or not?" I whispered.

Its nostrils flared. The metal around its throat whirred softly, gears clicking like something mechanical adjusting deep inside its body. It looked like a massive collar, but there was no chain attached to it. Its wings twitched as if in annoyance, but it didn't move.

It kept staring at me.

I didn't know what to do. Run further into the cave, just in case there was another exit? Try and communicate with the beast? Lie down and play dead?

Suddenly, the collar around its neck flared with light. Smoke rose from the dragon's nostrils as it shook its entire body.

We couldn't communicate. It didn't understand me. But I could see the pain in its eyes. It was in agony. The collar was hurting it.

My heart thumped painfully against my ribs. I didn't like to see anyone in pain, not even a huge cyborg beast who had kidnapped me and brought me to its lair.

More smoke, followed by a resigned snort. A deep rumble vibrated through the stone beneath me. Not quite a growl. Not quite a warning.

Without another sound, it lifted its massive weight and stretched its wings wide. The golden eyes lingered on me one last time. Then it pushed off from the cave floor and launched itself into the sky with a powerful beat of its wings.

And it was gone.

The entrance lay open. The cave was empty. I was alone.

For now.

For a few minutes, I stayed frozen, too scared to move. My body trembled. My brain refused to process what had just happened.

Eventually, survival instinct won out.

I stood on shaky legs, gripping my spear tight. My back ached from being carried like a ragdoll. My legs still felt like jelly, but I needed to move. Needed to explore. If there was a chance to get out of here, I had to find it.

The cave sloped upward towards the wide opening where the dragon had flown off. The mouth of the cave was massive, easily wide enough for the beast to pass through. I walked closer, squinting against the pale sunlight streaming inside.

When I reached the entrance, bile rose to my mouth.

The cliff dropped almost straight down. Hundreds of feet below, the crimson and gold forest stretched out like a sea of fire. Far in the distance, the Diamond Mountains sparkled, unreachable. The wind howled, tugging at my short hair.

There was no path down. No ledge. No handholds I could trust. Just smooth, sharp rock falling into nothing.

I backed away quickly, heart racing. That option was out. No climbing. No escape. I was trapped.

I rubbed my arms again, biting back a wave of helpless frustration. There had to be something. Anything. Maybe a second exit, one too small for the dragon to use.

I turned my attention back inside. I'd heard running water earlier, so I followed that sound until I found a spot where small trickles ran down the cave wall, pooling in a low basin underneath. A groove about as wide as my foot led the water away from there, further into the cave. A tiny stream.

The water seemed to be coming from above, hopefully pure rainwater filtered by the mountain. I dipped my finger in it and gave it a lick. No taste at all. That reassured me.

I drank my fill before following the little stream deeper into the cave. At the end of the wide cavern, it twisted and branched into a network of tunnels, far too narrow for the dragon. This could be my way out.

Bioluminescent moss glimmered along crystal formations, giving off a dim but steady light. I continued to follow the water. Even if this wouldn't lead outside, I couldn't lose my way. If I ventured into the other tunnels, I had to come up with a method to find my way back.

But did I even want that? Return to the dragon's

lair? It was safer in these small tunnels – until it blew fire into them and toasted me into a heap of ashes.

The further I walked, the warmer the air became, like there was heat pulsing from somewhere underground.

It was oddly peaceful, in a terrifying way.

That was when I heard it.

A tiny clicking sound, like claws on stone. Much more delicate than the sound a dragon would make, but larger than a mouse or rat.

I froze.

The noise came from one of the side tunnels, coming closer quickly. Then a faint scratching. And something small peeked out from behind a glowing crystal.

At first, I thought it was a lizard. But as it stepped – no, *waddled* – into the light, I blinked in disbelief.

It was a dragon. And nothing like the one that had abducted me.

A tiny, purple dragon. Its scales shimmered like polished amethyst. A single unicorn-like horn jutted from the centre of its round forehead, framed by two curled horns on either side. Chubby cheeks puffed slightly as it exhaled tiny curls of smoke from its nostrils. Its big, dark eyes blinked up at me, framed by delicate lashes that made it look entirely too adorable for its own good.

Spikes like little stegosaurus plates ran down its back, shrinking towards the stubby tail. Its bat-like wings fluttered once as it hovered briefly above the ground, tiny four-fingered claws tucked close to its round belly. Its hind legs ended in sharp talons that clicked softly against the stone as it landed.

The baby dragon tilted its head, blinked again, and let out a high-pitched tweet that was so sweet, I almost forgot where I was.

It took a step closer, not afraid. Just... curious.

"You have got to be kidding me," I whispered.

The tiny dragon let out another soft tweet, then turned around with a little wiggle of its stubby tail and trotted off, its claws clicking rhythmically on the stone. It moved surprisingly fast for such a round, wobbly creature.

I hesitated for half a second before following. What else was I going to do? Sit here and wait for its massive cousin to return? No thanks.

The little dragon led me back through the narrow tunnels, following the stream I had used as my guide. Soon we returned to the wide central chamber, the heart of the cave. The main lair.

The baby stopped in the middle of the open space and turned to look at me again, its big dark eyes wide with innocent curiosity. It flapped its tiny wings once and puffed a fresh spiral of smoke into the air.

I crouched down slowly, careful not to startle it. My heart raced, but not from fear. Not anymore. This one didn't seem dangerous. Adorable? Yes. Deadly? Not so far.

"Hey, little one," I whispered, keeping my voice soft

and even. "You're a whole lot cuter than your big scary friend, you know that?"

The baby blinked, tilting its head as if considering my words. Then it waddled closer, stopping just within arm's reach. It looked up at me expectantly, like it was waiting for something.

Very slowly, I reached out my hand, palm up. "You want a pet? Is that it?"

For a moment, it just stared. Then it shuffled forward and nudged my fingers with its soft, warm snout. A tiny exhale of warm air tickled my skin.

I couldn't help it. A breathless laugh escaped my throat. "Okay. You're ridiculously cute."

The little dragon chirped again and leaned into my hand as I gently scratched under its chin. The tiny scales there were smooth but slightly warm to the touch. As I stroked its chubby neck, its eyelids drooped and it let out a low, happy rumble, like a kitten purring.

At least someone here liked me.

"Do you understand me?" I asked softly. "Are you some kind of pet? A baby? Are you his...?"

The baby dragon lifted its head again and blinked at me, clearly not understanding a word. Its wings fluttered a little, but it stayed close.

I sat down properly, cross-legged on the stone floor, my spear close at hand just in case the big dragon returned, and kept petting the strange little creature. For the first time since I had arrived on this nightmare planet, I wasn't terrified. Not entirely, anyway.

"Well," I whispered, "at least I'm not completely alone."

It nuzzled against my hand in return. Warmth filled me and it had nothing to do with the heat exuding from the little dragon's nostrils. This felt good. A moment to breathe and relax. To remember that my life had not always been this scary – and that it wouldn't stay like this, hopefully. I just had to find a way to get home. Somehow. Somewhere. Then everything could return to normal. Summers spent at digs on Orkney or the Shetland Isles, winters full of collating research, writing papers, going to conferences, interpreting the finds made in the summer. In the evenings, sofa time with my cat. Occasionally, when I felt particularly social, craft nights in the church hall, filled with little old ladies who'd scoff at my crochet and tell me endless stories about their grandchildren.

I always thought my life was boring and ordinary.

Now I missed it.

The soft moment was shattered by a sudden gust of wind howling through the cave entrance. A deep, rasping growl echoed through the chamber. The baby dragon tweeted anxiously, snuggling against my thigh for comfort.

I jerked my head up just in time to see a huge shadow blot out the light. The massive dragon landed heavily at the entrance, its metal-fused wings folding awkwardly as it staggered forward.

Blood dripped from its side, painting a dark trail across the stone. More blood stained its torn wing, one of the metal implants sparking faintly as it limped inside.

The collar around its neck was no longer lit. Was that a crack on its surface?

My heart slammed into my throat.

It was back.

And it was hurt.

Pain.

Heat.

Smoke in my throat.

Metal claws at my mind.

I disobeyed. They scream inside my head.

It hurts. They don't stop. But it is less loud than usual.

I should have killed. I should have burned them.

I did not.

The small ones live. The ones they fear. The ones they hate.

I was told to kill and I did not.

Because I remembered.

A flicker. A scent.

Soft skin. Warm breath.

Small hands. A voice like light.

Not prey. Not enemy.

Different.

Mine.

The fire inside me stirs. Old. Faint.

From before the metal. Before the pain.

I fly back to my cave. To stone. To dark. To quiet.

My wing drags. My bones crack. My fire is weak.

Pain is everything.

But she is close.

I feel her.

I hear her breath beneath the stone.

The pain will return.

The chains will pull.

But for now... I breathe.

And I remember.

And I hope.

Her breath is close.

The tiny one is close too.

I smell them both.

The pain softens when I breathe her scent.

Familiar. New. Warm.

Alive.

I am not made for this. Not made for choice.

I obey. I kill. I burn.

But I did not.

Because of her.

The collar is cracked. Weak.

The chains pull, but they slip.

The metal screams, but I can ignore it. For now.

I drag my body inside.

The stone holds me. The dark cools my fire.

I move slowly. My broken wing scrapes the ground.

Sparks dance from torn metal. The pain claws at me, but I welcome it.

It reminds me I am still here.

I lift my head.

She sits near the little one.

The tiny one presses against her. Soft sounds. Smoke curls from its nose.

The female does not run.

Her eyes find mine. Wide. Shining.

I feel her fear. But also something else.

She says something. I do not understand.

I lower my head to the stone. My breath hisses through my teeth. The pain bites deep, but I hold still.

I watch her.

She watches me.

The tiny one chirps softly, curling its claws around her leg.

Safe. Small. Trusting.

The chains pull. The commands hiss.

Take her.

Kill her.

I do not move.

The fire inside me stirs.

Old.

Returning.

Alive.

I woke up with a start. Everything was dark. It had to be the middle of the night.

Something warm and soft was snuggled against my belly. Something large and not-so-soft pushed against my back.

I froze as yesterday's events rose from my memories.

Dragons.

Two of them.

And if I wasn't mistaken, I was sandwiched in the middle of them.

Fuck.

I must have fallen asleep while watching the big dragon, bloodied and injured, as he slept fitfully. I remembered how I'd felt both scared and helpless. Scared of him. Scared for him.

Meeting the baby dragon had proved that their species was not altogether bad. The little one had been nothing but cute, never tried to nip me or scratch me. All he'd wanted was cuddles. Maybe the big dragon wasn't all that different. He could have killed me when he'd first wrapped his claws around me. Could have eaten me in my sleep.

But he hadn't.

I listened to his breathing, deep yet ragged. I didn't think he'd sounded that way yesterday, before he'd come back injured.

How had that even happened? One of his wings had been shredded to pieces and there had been blood all over him, hinting at other, deeper injuries. Whatever had attacked him had to be *big*. Not something I ever wanted to encounter.

The little dragon nestled tighter against my stomach, letting out a sleepy chirp. I dared a small glance down at him. His tiny bat wings twitched in his sleep, his chubby cheeks rising and falling with every soft puff of smoke from his nostrils. He was cuteness wrapped in scales, but my favourite part of him was the unicorn horn. I'd always loved unicorns. I couldn't help it after growing up in Scotland, a country that had the unicorn as its national animal.

Adorable little traitor. He clearly had no fear of the massive monster behind me. Maybe I shouldn't either. Or maybe the baby just didn't know any better.

The warmth radiating from behind me was almost soothing if I managed to forget what it belonged to. I could feel his slow, heavy breathing, the faint mechanical whir that accompanied every exhale. Occasionally, a faint crackle would sound somewhere deep inside his chest, like dying embers struggling to reignite.

I twisted my head slowly, carefully, just enough to peek over my shoulder.

He was still lying where I'd last seen him. That meant I had somehow moved closer in my sleep.

His huge body filled a good part of the cave's central chamber, wings half-folded, claws twitching slightly in his restless sleep. The metal around his throat still looked cracked, a faint, dull glow pulsing inside the damaged collar. Blood crusted along his torn wing and side.

His breathing hitched for a moment, as if some pain jolted him even in sleep. A soft, broken growl rumbled through the cave, so deep I felt it more than heard it.

I swallowed hard. What had happened to him out there? What kind of battle had done this to something so powerful?

And why did I feel... sorry for him?

He had taken me. Stolen me. Trapped me here like some kind of prize.

But something told me that if he truly wanted me dead, I wouldn't be here to question it.

And when had *it* become *he*?

I didn't even know if the dragon was male. Yes, he was huge and scary, but it didn't mean he had to be male. Still, something told me he was.

I gently stroked the tiny dragon's smooth scales. He snuggled in tighter, his little claws curling into my shirtless stomach. I couldn't help but smile despite the fear still gnawing at the edges of my mind.

"You're trusting, aren't you?" I whispered softly. "I hope you're right about him."

The large dragon's breathing shifted again, his huge tail giving a slow, dragging twitch. His head lay only a few feet away now, turned slightly in my direction. Even asleep, his golden eyes fluttered open briefly, locking on me for a heartbeat before closing again.

I held my breath.

He didn't move. Didn't growl. Just... watched. And then drifted back into sleep.

Whatever programming or instinct made him grab me in the first place, it was like something inside him was fighting against it. The longer I stayed, the more that thought settled into my gut.

He was broken. Controlled. And somehow, I had become part of that crack in his chains.

I wasn't sure if that made me safer... or in even more danger.

When dawn rose and tinged the cave in pale pink light, the dragon woke with a sneeze.

It was a strange sound. Half rumble, half wheeze, with a little puff of smoke escaping his nostrils that drifted lazily into the still air. The baby dragon snuggled against me chirped and wiggled its tiny limbs, but didn't wake.

I lay frozen for a second, bracing for... well,

anything. But the big dragon didn't lash out. Instead, he lifted his massive head slowly, as if every movement cost him energy. The golden glow in his eyes flared faintly, landing on me again. Watching.

His gaze felt heavy but not aggressive. Just... present. Curious.

I swallowed, trying to keep my voice even. "Good morning?"

No reaction, obviously. What was I expecting? A polite reply? A bow? Maybe a little tea and bickies while we chatted about why exactly he'd kidnapped me?

His gaze flicked briefly to the tiny dragon curled against my stomach, then back to my face. If I didn't know better, I'd have called that expression almost thoughtful. Or protective. Like he was pleased the baby was safe with me.

His breath rattled again. The faint hum of machinery beneath his skin shifted and clicked, like struggling gears barely holding together. His injuries still looked bad. Deep gashes where metal met flesh. Torn wings. That cracked collar faintly pulsing with unstable energy.

He looked to be in bad shape. Did dragons heal fast or was this going to take weeks or even months?

I licked my lips and sat up carefully, dislodging the baby dragon just enough to free my hands. It chirped once but settled right back down, its head resting on my lap. I rubbed its little snout absentmindedly while forcing my brain to keep up with my mouth.

"You're hurt," I said softly. "You... need help."

The dragon tilted his head. The collar around his throat sparked slightly. No understanding in his eyes, but no hostility either.

I took a careful breath and scooted a tiny bit closer. My heart pounded so loud I was sure he could hear it. "I don't know if you can understand me. But if you can, you have to know I'm not your enemy."

Still no response. But still no attack.

Another breath. Another slow shuffle forward. Closer now, almost close enough to reach him.

I glanced at his injured wing, at the torn membranes and exposed metal. The wounds didn't look fresh anymore, but they hadn't been cleaned either. Infection was likely, even in an alien. That collar looked even worse – like it could explode or fry his brain at any moment.

He watched every movement, his massive head turning slightly as I leaned in.

"I just want to look," I whispered. "I'm not going to hurt you."

The tiny dragon chirped softly, sensing my unease. I ignored it for the moment, fully focusing on its big companion instead.

I reached out my hand.

Slowly. Carefully.

And touched his wing.

The texture surprised me. Warm, leathery, but not slimy. The edge of the torn membrane quivered under my fingers, as if even this gentle contact sent a ripple of pain through him. His body tensed, a deep rumble vibrating in his chest. I froze, heart hammering.

But he didn't pull away.

He let me touch him.

"I'm sorry," I whispered, almost to myself. "I wish I knew how to help."

The dragon blinked slowly. A breath of hot air washed over me, not threatening, almost... tired.

I lowered my hand and leaned back slightly, giving him space again. "You could have killed me. But you didn't."

I wasn't sure why I said it aloud. Maybe I needed him to know I recognized that. Or maybe I just needed to hear myself say it.

He blinked again.

Then, unexpectedly, he lowered his head further until his massive snout hovered barely inches above me. His breath was hot and sharp with a faint metallic scent, but I didn't flinch.

We stared at each other for a long moment, neither of us daring to move.

I reached out again, slower this time, and gently placed my hand against his snout.

The scales were warm beneath my palm. Smooth. Strange. Real.

"You're not a monster," I whispered. "Are you?"

The dragon closed his eyes.

And exhaled a deep, heavy breath against my chest.

The moment stretched between us, heavy and strange. His massive head remained still beneath my hand, his eyes closed, his breath warm against my chest. He wasn't just tolerating me. He was trusting me.

The tiny dragon chirped again and wiggled closer, its soft scales pressing against my side. The little one clearly had no fear. Somehow, that helped. If this baby trusted him, maybe I could too.

But my gaze kept drifting to the collar around his neck.

It sparked again. A sharp, angry pulse of light rippled through the cracked metal, followed by a faint hiss. The skin beneath the metal was blistered and raw. The damage wasn't just on the outside. Whatever that thing was, it was hurting him from the inside too.

Every instinct screamed that I should stay back. That touching anything like that could kill me instantly.

But I couldn't just sit here and watch while this thing tortured him.

"I don't know what they did to you," I whispered, my voice trembling. "But this... this isn't right."

The collar sparked again, and his body twitched with a sharp intake of breath. I flinched but didn't pull my hand away.

I glanced at the seams of the metal. There was a faint gap where the crack had widened. Just big enough for me to maybe pry it open. Or break it entirely.

If I was careful.

If I was lucky.

And if this wasn't going to blow my head off.

I let out a long, shaky breath. "Okay, Hazel," I

muttered under my breath, "this is either the dumbest or bravest thing you've ever done."

Very slowly, I got to my feet and reached for the damaged collar.

The dragon's golden eyes opened, watching me. Not aggressive. Curious. Waiting.

I swallowed. "I'm going to help you. If you let me."

Another small spark jumped from the collar as if in warning.

Maybe I shouldn't do this with my bare hands. I searched the cave floor for my spear. With a sigh, I broke it in half. Goodbye, little weapon. You wouldn't have been of any use anyway. Not against this dragon and not against the monsters down in the valley.

I stood by the dragon's neck, the collar now very close. My fingers hovered over the metal, feeling the faint hum of energy beneath my skin. My pulse raced.

"I'm going to try and wedge it open," I warned the dragon. "I really hope this won't hurt you. Or me."

The baby dragon watched me with those big dark eyes, as if sensing the tension. Its tiny head tilted, and it let out a soft, questioning chirp.

"I know," I whispered to the little one. "It's insane. But maybe insane is what we need right now."

I pushed the spear parts into the opening and took a deep breath.

This could go very, very wrong.

TYVARON

Pain.

The stone no longer calms the pain.

Wing on fire.

Neck so tight.

Burning everywhere.

But she is here with me.

Her scent soothes.

She is light.

She has no fear. She is close, touching me.

She split her twig in two. I wonder what she intends.

I do not need a toothpick.

She leans against my neck.

Pain.

Crack.

The metal screams.

The collar splits.

For a moment, everything burns. Sparks fill my

vision. My body convulses. The chains pull. Hard. Voices in the distance. Commands I do not obey.

But then-

Silence.

The weight lifts.

The metal inside my mind peels away, like claws slipping free from my skull. The commands fade. The voices fall silent.

I breathe.

Deep.

The scent fills me.

Soft skin. Warm breath.

Her.

I see her. Not just shape. Not just prey.

Female.

Small hands. Gentle touch.

She stands before me, shaking. Brave. Stupid. Glorious.

I remember more.

I was not always this. Not always metal and fire. There was a time before the pain. Before the chains. Before I was turned into a weapon.

My mind clears. My thoughts sharpen.

Language returns, stumbling like a newborn beast. Heavy. Strange. But mine.

She spoke. I heard her voice before. Words I could not grasp.

Now... I almost can.

There is an echo inside me, of someone I used to

be. Not a beast. Someone more like her. But it fades, that echo, until it is almost out of grasp.

The little one chirps by her side. Safe. Trusting.

She freed me.

The collar cracks fully. The last lock snaps with a soft hiss. It falls to the ground. Gone. The weight is gone.

I lift my head slowly, carefully. My body aches. My wings drag behind me like broken banners.

But I see her.

Her.

I open my mouth. My voice is raw, unused.

Deep. Rough.

"Mine," I say.

Her eyes widen. She gasps.

I breathe again.

Alive.

Free.

"Mine," he said.

The word rumbled through the cave like distant thunder, low and rough, lapping at my skin in a way that made every nerve stand at attention.

I froze.

He had spoken.

Not growled. Not roared. Spoken.

That sound, that word, shouldn't have been able to come from a maw like his, full of razor-sharp teeth. But it had. I was sure of it. I hadn't just imagined it... right?

He looked at me, golden eyes wide and unblinking, as if waiting for something. As if the very act of saying that single word had taken everything he had.

I swallowed hard, my mouth suddenly dry. "You... you can talk?"

No answer. Just that heavy stare. His head remained low, his injured wings limp behind him, but there was something in his eyes that hadn't been there before. Focus. Awareness. Intelligence.

The collar lay shattered on the ground between us, a twisted piece of metal sparking faintly. I glanced at it, then back at him.

"You're free," I whispered. "I broke it. You're free now, aren't you?"

He didn't reply, but I could see it. Feel it. The way he watched me had changed. Less like an animal. More like... something thinking. Processing.

My heart pounded. "You said... mine." I forced out a shaky laugh. "What does that mean? Do you mean you... I mean, me? Or... is that just a word you remember? Or are you speaking a different language and it just sounded like it?"

His nostrils flared softly. A puff of warm air brushed my skin. He shifted his weight slightly, claws scraping against the stone, but made no move to threaten me.

The tiny dragon chirped and flapped its little wings, landing on my lap once again. Completely unbothered by any of this. I would have been very surprised if he had been aware of what was going on.

I kept talking, because silence was scarier. "Listen, big guy. I appreciate that you're not trying to eat me right now. Really. Huge improvement. But I have no idea what's going on here. I don't even know your name." My voice shook. "Do you have a name?"

The dragon's mouth parted slightly. His throat worked, like forming words was difficult. Foreign.

"Ty... va..." His voice cracked. Rougher than before, strained. "Tyvaron."

I blinked. "Tyvaron," I repeated softly. "Is that you? Your name?"

He blinked once, as if reconsidering. "No."

"Then what is it? Your kind? Your species?"

Again, he blinked. "No."

In my head, I ran through other options. Job title. Unlikely. Honorific. Maybe. Rank. Perhaps?

"Is it what others call you?"

A slow, deliberate nod followed. Stiff, but unmistakable.

Relief surged through me, mingled with a dizzying wave of adrenaline. I wasn't sure whether I wanted to cry, scream, or laugh hysterically.

"Okay. Then I guess I shall call you that as well, until you tell me your actual name. Tyvaron." My voice trembled. "I'm Hazel."

Another slow blink. His massive head tilted slightly. "Ha-zzzzzel," he rasped, the word strange in his mouth but clear enough to make my stomach flip.

I let out a breathless laugh. "Well. That's a start."

The baby dragon chirped happily, as if pleased with the introductions, and rubbed its little snout against my arm. I absently stroked its tiny head, unable to take my eyes off Tyvaron.

This creature, this beast who had kidnapped me and carried me to this cave, was no longer just a monster.

He was someone.

And for reasons I couldn't begin to understand, I had just become part of whatever he was now.

Tyvaron shifted slightly as if to be more comfortable, but then hissed in pain. Steam poured from his nostrils. The collar may have been gone, but that didn't mean he was suddenly all healed and well.

"How can I help?" I asked. "What can I do to lessen your pain?"

He cocked his head at me, as if he was confused.

"Help?" he repeated slowly, cautiously.

"Yes, help. You're in pain. I don't like that. Yes, you may have kidnapped me and taken me here, but you've not done anything else to harm me. I might be able to see past the abduction-by-dragon thing if you promise not to eat me. Sorry, I'm rambling. I do that when I'm nervous."

I pointed at his torn wing. The blood had mostly dried but there were a few spots where it was still seeping.

"You're injured. Is there something I can do? Would water help, maybe?"

He tilted his massive head again, blinking as if trying to process my words. His eyes narrowed, not with anger but with concentration.

"Water," he repeated, the word rough but clearer this time.

I nodded, encouraged. "Yes. Water. For cleaning." I mimed washing with my hands, hoping that might help get my meaning across.

His gaze flicked briefly to the thin stream trickling

along the cave wall, then returned to me. Another slow breath escaped him, a soft rumble vibrating through his chest. It wasn't approval exactly, but it wasn't a refusal either.

"Alright. Water it is." I exhaled shakily and stood, forcing my knees to stop trembling. "You just... stay there. Try not to explode or die while I'm gone, okay?"

He watched me closely as I crossed the cavern. The baby dragon trailed after me like an eager toddler, chirping softly with each tiny hop.

When I reached the little pool where the water gathered, I paused, glancing around for something to carry it in. I came up empty. All I had was my hands.

Bloody hell. This was going to take a while.

I returned to Tyvaron slowly, carrying my very limited supply of water. I had cupped it directly in my hands, careful not to spill too much as I crossed the uneven stone floor.

By the time I reached him again, most of it had already leaked through my fingers. This wasn't sustainable.

I glanced around desperately for something else, anything that could hold water better than my hands. My gaze landed on a cluster of smooth crystal shards protruding from the wall nearby. One of them had broken off and was lying on the ground, shaped like a shallow bowl. It sparkled faintly under the dim light as if to say, use me.

I picked it up carefully. "Okiedokie," I muttered, "Let's try this.

The improvised container worked surprisingly well. The smooth surface would hold the water long enough for me to gently pour it over Tyvaron's wounds without soaking myself in the process.

I knelt beside him again, clutching the improvised crystal bowl, my hands still trembling slightly. Tyvaron's huge eyes followed my every move, patient but alert.

"Okay, big guy," I whispered. "Let's try this again."

I gently poured the water close to the edge of one of the largest gashes along his wing. The skin twitched beneath my touch, but he didn't pull away. Just a deep, slow exhale warmed my face, accompanied by the faintest hum of mechanical clicks somewhere inside his chest.

"You're doing great," I whispered, forcing a little smile as much for myself as for him.

The baby dragon waddled closer and watched me work, blinking those enormous eyes with the kind of innocent curiosity only something completely oblivious to danger could have.

I refilled the bowl and picked up some of the bioluminescent moss to use as a sponge. Tyvaron stared at the moss for a bit, as if he wasn't sure why I'd chosen it, but didn't complain.

I worked methodically, wiping away the crusted blood and grime, carefully avoiding the places where metal met flesh. The wounds themselves were fascinating in a morbid sort of way – his body was clearly trying to heal around the implants, but they'd been damaged too. Twisted. Burnt in some places.

Whoever did this to him hadn't just attached these pieces to his body. They'd forced them into him. The thought made my stomach turn.

"This shouldn't have happened to you," I whispered softly.

Tyvaron made a low sound. Not a growl. Not a purr. More like a rumble of... acknowledgment. Or maybe comfort. I wasn't sure. But it made me keep going.

By the time I felt like I'd made some progress, my back hurt and my hands were covered in dragon blood. I sat back on my heels and let out a long breath.

"That's the best I can do for now," I said, studying my work. The wounds were still ugly, but cleaner. Less raw. The risk of infection, at least, should be a little lower now.

Tyvaron shifted his head slightly, lowering it until his snout hovered just a few inches from my face. His eyes locked onto mine. The proximity sent a shiver through me, but I didn't move.

His breath washed over me. Warm. Steady.

"You're... different now," I said softly. "Since I took that collar off. You're thinking. You're... awake."

His head tilted.

"You feel... clearer, don't you?" My voice shook, but I kept talking. "You can understand more. Speak more. Think more. That thing... it was controlling you."

Tyvaron blinked slowly. His jaw moved slightly, lips parting as though trying to shape words again.

I waited, heart hammering.

"Less... chains," he rasped, voice hoarse but unmistakably deliberate. "More... me."

A thrill of astonishment ran through me. "Yes!" I smiled despite myself. "Exactly. You're you again."

His chest rumbled. A strange sound. Like an echo of a purr, though still raw and mechanical beneath.

"And you're not going to hurt me, right?" I whispered.

Tyvaron paused. His eyes narrowed just slightly, then softened. His voice came again, rough but firmer this time.

"No. Hazzzel... mine."

The word made my breath catch. His possessive tone sent a shiver down my spine that was equal parts terrifying and... something else I wasn't ready to analyse.

I swallowed hard and forced a nervous laugh. "Yeah, you keep saying that."

The baby dragon chirped, oblivious, happily curling around my thigh like we were all old friends sharing tea.

I didn't know what I was anymore. A prisoner? A guest? Something in between?

But in this moment, as utterly insane as it was, I didn't feel like prey.

I felt... safe.

For now.

Hazel.

Her voice is soft. Her touch careful. My skin burns where her fingers were, but not from pain.

This is new. Strange. Dangerous.

Nobody has ever done this before.

I remember their touches. It hurt. They transformed me without taking note of my pain.

Hazel is different. She is kind. She helps.

She talks to me. I only understand parts of it.

I know what I was made for. Obey. Kill. Destroy.

But I did not kill.

I remember the moment. The command screamed in my head. The small ones stood before me. The old prey. The new prey.

And I stopped.

Because of her.

Because of the scent that had already reached me.

Because of the light she carries, like a flame against the metal inside me.

The chains have loosened. Not gone, but weaker.

Less chains. More me.

She looks at me with wide eyes. Afraid, yes. But not like before. Now her fear is thin, wrapped in something warmer.

She speaks to me. Words that once were only noise now carry meaning. Not all. But some.

"You're not going to hurt me, right?"

I understand.

I could. Easily. I always could.

But I will not.

Never. Not her.

I shape the word again. Rough. Possessive. True.

"Mine."

Her breath hitches. The scent of her pulse sharpens. She trembles. But she does not run.

I do not want her to run.

I do not want her to leave.

I want... more.

The little one chirps and curls against her leg. The little one trusts her. I trust the little one. It is the innocent one. The one they did not find. The one they did not change. The little one means hope.

I close my eyes. The stone beneath me holds my weight. The wounds throb. My wing drags. My strength is thin.

But I feel something I have not felt in... how long? I do not know. Time is broken.

Hope.

I was exhausted.

The adrenaline had finally burned out, leaving behind a hollow kind of fatigue that made my limbs feel heavy. I sat beside Tyvaron's massive head, absently petting the little dragon curled against my lap.

Everything around me still felt unreal. Surreal. Impossible.

He'd spoken. He had a name. Or at least, something close to a name.

And somehow, I wasn't dead.

I was also hungry. But there was nothing edible in the cave. Soon, I'd ask Tyvaron in the hope that he would understand. And that he wouldn't end up offering me raw meat. Maybe the tiny dragon had a food source he was willing to share with me.

I looked down at him, nestled against me like an overgrown cat. He chirped softly, eyelids drooping, perfectly content in this insane situation.

"You're awfully trusting," I whispered. "I hope you're right."

Then I felt it.

A strange sensation prickled across my skin. Not a sound, not a movement exactly, but an awareness. Like being watched by something just out of sight.

I froze. My eyes darted towards the far end of the cave where shadows clung to the walls. The faint glow from the crystals didn't quite reach that corner, but I thought I saw... movement.

Something small.

My grip tightened on the baby dragon, and he lifted his head, blinking sleepily into the shadows.

The soft clicking noise came first. Then a shape stepped into view.

A little smaller than the little dragon. Pale silver. A nimble body – a cross between a monkey and a cat – covered in silver feathers. Almost glowing. Four tails flicked behind it in slow, deliberate rhythm. Three large eyes, too big for its delicate face, studied me with a curious, unreadable expression.

Another monkey-cat strolled into the cave, this one golden. Then a third.

My first instinct was panic. They didn't exactly look scary, but they were invading a dragon's lair as if they had nothing to fear. That made my breath grow faster as I prepared to act. But before I could scramble back, the tiny dragon in my lap let out a cheerful trill and hopped off, waddling towards the newcomers like greeting old friends.

I blinked, stunned.

The baby dragon rubbed his little head against one of the small creatures' side, releasing a happy puff of smoke. The creature leaned down, gently pressing its delicate hands to the little dragon's back in what almost looked like an affectionate gesture.

They knew each other.

The tension in my chest eased slightly. My fingers unclenched. Whatever these creatures were, they weren't here to hurt him. Or me. At least not yet.

The silver one tilted its head, studying me with large, dark eyes, one above the two others. Its long tails elegantly moved above it in repeating spirals, almost hypnotising.

I *felt* its attention on me like a cloak being thrown around my shoulders.

I couldn't hear anything. No words. No sound.

But I felt it.

A strange warmth bloomed in my chest. A ripple of calm, like a hand resting lightly over my heart. Not words exactly. Not thoughts. More like... an impression.

Safe.

I let out a shaky breath. "You're not here to hurt me, are you?"

The creature didn't respond, but it took another slow step forward, lifting its hands in what I hoped was a universal sign of peace.

The baby dragon chirped again and rubbed against it like a happy cat.

I glanced nervously at Tyvaron. His eyes were open now, following the creatures with clear aware-ness. But he didn't growl. Didn't lash out.

He was watching.

Just like me.

The three beings slowly approached Tyvaron. I almost let out a sigh of relief. They weren't here for me. They had come for him.

"Can you help him?" I blurted before I could stop myself.

The creatures paused for a moment, their large dark eyes turning towards me. I tensed, unsure if I had made a mistake by speaking, but then that strange wave of calm washed over me again. Not words. Not thoughts. Just... reassurance.

They moved closer to Tyvaron, their movements smooth and fluid, tails flicking softly behind them. The baby dragon trotted along beside them, happily chirp-ing, utterly unfazed by any of this.

The smallest of the three stopped right beside Tyvaron's head. One golden hand reached out and rested gently on his snout, right between his eyes.

Tyvaron remained perfectly still. His breathing was slow, steady, controlled. If he was worried at all, he didn't show it.

A soft hum filled the air. Barely audible. I wasn't sure if it was real or just inside my head, but it vibrated gently in my chest, like the low hum of a distant power line.

The other two creatures moved towards the broken

remains of the collar. They circled it, examining the shattered pieces like curious scientists. They were studying the thing that had enslaved him.

"What are you doing?" I whispered, not expecting an answer but needing to say something.

The one beside Tyvaron lifted its hand slightly, as though inviting me to stay calm. Another ripple of reassurance pressed gently into my mind. Peace. Trust.

I swallowed hard, watching as they continued to move with deliberate care, examining Tyvaron but never harming him. Whatever they were doing, Tyvaron allowed it. That, more than anything, convinced me to stay quiet.

Maybe they *were* here to help.

Or at least, I hoped so.

The creature resting its hand on Tyvaron's snout closed its enormous eyes. The faint hum grew a little stronger, resonating through the air like a long forgotten song.

Tyvaron didn't move. His body remained still, but his golden eyes slowly drifted shut as well. A deep rumble passed through him, not in pain this time, but something else. A surrender.

The air itself seemed to thicken around us. I wasn't hearing anything exactly, but I *felt* it. Something was happening, even though I didn't know what it was.

The other two creatures moved closer, forming a loose half-circle around his head. Their tails swayed gently, in unison, like some strange ritual. Their breathing synchronized, and the hum deepened.

The baby dragon, still nestled against my side, chirped softly but didn't seem alarmed. He rested his head on my thigh and let out a little sigh, as if everything happening was perfectly normal.

I wished I shared his confidence.

"What are you doing to him?" I whispered, even though I knew they wouldn't answer.

The humming intensified, vibrating faintly through the stone beneath me. My stomach tightened, but Tyvaron remained still. His massive body relaxed more fully than I'd ever seen since the moment I met him. The tension in his limbs softened. His injured wing settled against the ground without twitching.

Then I felt it.

A pulse.

Like a shockwave of something ancient and heavy rippling through the cave, but not physical. Mental.

Tyvaron gasped, his breath rattling hard through his chest.

His golden eyes snapped open.

But they were different.

Clearer.

Sharper.

And somehow... *more human.*

He stared ahead, blinking slowly as though seeing his surroundings for the first time. His gaze swept past the pale creatures, past the little dragon, and landed directly on me.

"Hazel," he said, his voice stronger now. Still rough, but deliberate.

I couldn't breathe.

The change in Tyvaron's eyes was undeniable. Not just aware. Not just intelligent. But... awake. Like something vast and ancient had finally cracked open inside him.

The creatures stepped back as the hum softened. One by one, they lowered their hands and slowly withdrew from his side, their tails still swaying in synchronized arcs. The air grew lighter again, the thick pressure lifting from the cave.

Tyvaron's massive chest expanded as he drew in a long, deliberate breath. His gaze swept across the cave, scanning everything cautiously. The crystals. The stream. The broken collar. Me.

His eyes landed on me and held.

"Hazel," he said again.

It was only one word, one name, but he said it with such clarity that I knew things had changed.

"Tyvaron," I whispered, my voice breaking slightly. "What did they do to you?"

Tyvaron blinked once, slow and steady. His eyes shifted towards the creatures, then back to me.

He inhaled deeply. "They helped," he rasped, voice still rough but growing stronger. "They... woke me."

That was exactly what I'd thought. He looked so much more aware, even though his injuries persisted.

I swallowed hard at the thought of him being in pain. "Who are they?"

He was silent for a moment, as if reaching for words he hadn't used in a long time. His gaze flicked to the feathered aliens again, as though receiving input I couldn't hear.

"Old ones," he said finally. "Chii."

"Chii," I repeated softly, the word strange on my tongue. "They're what, your allies?"

His head dipped once. "Not anymore. They fear me. Us. But now... everything has changed. They hope. Because I showed mercy. I started to break my chains."

I glanced at the pale creatures again. They stood still, their huge dark eyes unblinking, observing me without any sign of threat.

"And the little one?" I whispered, looking down at the baby dragon beside me. "He knows them?"

"Yes," Tyvaron answered, his voice clearer with each word. "She is innocent. Not tainted like me. A reminder of what I used to be."

"Wait, she?"

Oops. I shouldn't have assumed.

"She." Was that amusement in his voice?

The baby dragon chirped, as if affirming his words.

I exhaled slowly, my mind spinning. "So they're helping you because you... showed mercy? How? When? Because you didn't eat me?"

He was quiet again, breathing heavily. Then a low rumble vibrated through him.

"No. I broke commands. Disobeyed my masters. I am... different." His voice dropped to a softer rasp. "You make me different. You make me remember."

The words made me hold my breath.

Me? I made him remember?

Before I could respond, one of the Chii lifted a four-fingered hand – not towards me, but towards Tyvaron. He closed his eyes and inhaled deeply, as if receiving something more from them. Another ripple of that strange, invisible hum spread through the air. But this time, it wasn't oppressive. It was... light.

"They give pieces back," Tyvaron whispered. "Pieces I lost."

He paused. Then opened his eyes again – and this time, they burned even brighter.

"I remember... everything."

TYVARON

I woke in pieces.

The world was wrong. Too large. Too loud. Too sharp.

My body was heavy. Alien. My limbs did not respond as they once had. My hands – no, not hands. Claws. Long. Curved. My tail dragged behind me, unsteady, much bigger and heavier than it should have been.

I tried to sit up. My wings twitched, folding awkwardly against my sides, as if they had suddenly grown and changed. Bone and metal grinding together.

Panic clawed at my mind.

Where was I?

The chamber around me pulsed with faint light. Machinery hummed beneath the metal floor. Cables slithered like veins across the walls. I recognized none of it.

But I remembered myself.

My name. My people. My form.

Draquari.

I was-

The memory slipped through my fingers like water. Blurry shapes. Faces. Voices calling my name. My kin, my family. Fading.

A sharp, searing pain exploded at my throat. I roared, the sound foreign and terrible, filling the chamber with heat and smoke.

Something tightened around my scales. Cold metal. A collar.

It bit into my flesh, burning as energy pulsed through it, silencing my thoughts. My head snapped downward, chest heaving.

Comply.

The voice echoed inside my skull. Mechanical. Cold. Other.

Comply. Obey.

I writhed, trying to resist. My mind screamed.

I am not this.

I am free.

I am not –

Pain again. Blinding. Shattering.

The memories slipped further. Faces faded. Names blurred.

Another voice entered my mind. Softer. Familiar. My own voice, or something like it.

Survive.

I breathed. Forced myself still. The pain lessened. I could think again.

They left me alone for a while. The collar loosened. But it remained around my neck, a reminder that everything had changed. I was no longer myself. No longer free.

The next cycle, I saw them. The small ones. The masters.

So much smaller than me, especially now that they had transformed me into something monstrous, but so much more powerful. They could tighten the collar, make it burn with fierce pain, make me scream until blackness took me.

And they were always watching.

Judging.

Testing.

I would resist at first. Then I learned not to.

So much pain. Wounds. Scars.

Time passed. My old life faded. I could barely remember anything of what I used to be.

I was so different now. Huge wings, supported by metal. Claws so sharp they could tear through diamond. Horns on my head, curled and ugly. A face I did not want to look at. And inside me, fire, burning, smoking, waiting to pour out of me.

One cycle, the masters let me outside. I blinked at the sunshine. The air was full of scents. They didn't let me enjoy the moment. There was a perch filled with smaller beings. Afraid. Huddled. Screaming in fear at the sight of me.

Eliminate.

The command vibrated through my skull like a

hammer blow.

I staggered forward. My claws scraped the ground. My wings twitched. I tried to stop. To scream. To beg.

The collar burned again.

Obey.

I lunged. The first was small. Fragile. I tore through them with ease.

Their screams rang in my ears.

My mind recoiled. Revulsion surged through me. *This is wrong. This is wrong.*

But the pain eased.

The collar approved.

Good boy.

Another kill. And another. Each death pulled something out of me. Not just guilt. Not just horror. Something deeper. Pieces of who I was.

The words I once knew faded further. My name grew distant. My past dulled.

Comply. Obey. Destroy.

Time dissolved.

More kills. More missions. More pain when I resisted. Less pain when I obeyed.

The memories slipped like fog in the sun, leaving behind only the fire in my chest, the hunger in my belly, and the voices in my mind.

Until nothing remained but the chains.

I breathed.

Fully. Deeply.

For the first time in what felt like forever, the air filled my chest without chains tightening around my mind.

The memories burned inside me. They had returned all at once, like a dam breaking. Crushing. Overwhelming.

My past. Before I became an abomination. And the rotations since everything changed. The senseless violence. The killings. The pain of who I was. The horror of what they made me.

And yet... I was awake.

Hazel sat beside me, watching carefully, her scent wrapping around my thoughts like a warm current. The little one rested against her leg, chirping softly, trusting completely. The chii stood nearby, their task complete, their wide eyes calm but wary.

I lowered my head towards Hazel, speaking slowly. Clearly.

"They made me."

Her breath caught. "Who did?"

"The same people who put you on this planet. The game makers." My voice rasped, unfamiliar with full words, but stronger now. "I was not born like this. I was... created. Built. Changed."

Her brows knit together. "But you were... someone before."

I nodded slowly. "Yes. Before. I had a name. A face. A body not unlike yours. I had wings then, but they were much smaller." My chest tightened. "I do not remember my name. Not yet. They took it."

Hazel's voice softened. "How?"

"Each time I killed, they took more." My claws flexed against the stone. "Every mission. Every target. Every order I obeyed pulled more of me away." My wings twitched, causing sharp pain to spread through them. I had to take care of these injuries soon. "Until only the weapon remained."

Her eyes glistened, but she didn't look away. She was not afraid of me. Not anymore. That, more than anything, gave me strength.

"The collar controlled me," I continued. "Pain when I resisted. Silence when I obeyed. The others... the other tyvarin, they still wear their chains. Still serve."

Hazel's breath hitched. "Others like you?"

"Many. Some are still here on Kalumbu, but most were taken elsewhere. Sent to wage war against others." My voice darkened. "We were their greatest creation. Their army. Built from warriors taken across worlds. Altered. Rewritten. Some surrendered. Some fought. I rebelled at first." My throat tightened. "But the pain... the pain always won."

Hazel whispered, almost to herself. "But not anymore."

"No." I exhaled. "Not anymore."

She looked at the chii, then back at me. "They helped you."

"Yes. I knew about the chii from the little one. She gets into places I don't. While I was trapped in this cave, waiting for the next command from my masters, she explored the world, met the chii, told me everything she witnessed. I think she was the first step to finding myself again."

Hazel scratched the little one's head, who leaned into her touch. "Does she have a name?"

"Yes, but it is not in a language like the ones we speak. If I had to translate it, it would be something like shiny-ruby-in-a-glittering-cave-beneath-deep-mountains. But no, that barely touches the true meaning of her name."

"Ruby." She looked down at the little one. "Is it alright if I call you Ruby?"

I translated the question into dragon-speak. The little one chirped happily.

"Yes," I said with a smile.

When had I last smiled? Or even attempted to do so?

It felt strange. Like my jaw was making movements it wasn't supposed to.

Hazel focused back on me. "I've been meaning to ask, how is it you understand me? How can we talk to each other?"

"They must have given you a translator implant. I also have one, part of the many things they implanted into my body." I shuddered in disgust. It was a miracle she didn't despise me for what I was. An abomination created to kill. That's all I was.

"An implant?" She grasped her head as if searching for the blasted thing. "Where?"

"I am not sure. It depends on the species. But do not worry. They are harmless."

"Harmless," she scoffed. "They implanted something into me without my permission. That's not harmless."

Her eyes widened. "I am so sorry. You must think I'm so insensitive after you've just told me that they did all sorts of unspeakable things to you. I shouldn't complain about it."

"No. You should. Any invasion of our bodies is equally wrong. Whether it's a translator implant or artificial fire."

Her eyes got even wider. "You were not born that way?"

I sighed. "It is my most terrible weapon. The masters delight in forcing me to burn others until there is nothing left but ash in the wind. Earlier, they gave me that same command. But I refused."

"Who did they want you to burn?"

"There was a group. A shuttle crew. And a male serpent, with a female by his side. They were enemies of the game makers. I was ordered to destroy them." My voice darkened. "I nearly did."

Hazel blinked, frowning. "A serpent?"

My claws flexed against the stone. "I saw something familiar in him. In all of them. They were not the usual contestants in the masters' foul games, unaware, running from monsters, dying alone. The game makers were desperate for them to die. These ones fought back. And I... stopped."

Hazel swallowed. "You let them live."

"I disobeyed." My voice softened. "For the first time. And that was when the chii saw there was still something left of me worth saving."

Something about the memory nagged at the back of my mind. Wait...

"The female who was with the serpent. She was like you. That is why I did not burn them all. I remember now. She reminded me of you. I think she may have been from your world."

My mind spun.

Every time I thought I understood what was happening, the world shifted again.

Tyvaron had once been like me. Humanoid. Free. Someone. Then these game makers had taken him. Broken him. Turned him into... this. Not a monster, not truly. A weapon they had programmed and twisted until only tiny pieces of who he once was remained.

And somehow, against all odds, he was clawing his way back.

I looked at him. His massive head hovered close, golden eyes clear and bright. But behind them I saw exhaustion. Pain. And something else I hadn't expected. Vulnerability.

"The other human," I whispered. "The woman. What happened to her?"

He nodded slowly. "She boarded the ship with the serpent male. They escaped."

I sucked in a breath. Another human. Someone from Earth, like me. I wasn't alone. There were others who'd survived this nightmare. My throat tightened painfully at the thought.

"She was safe?" My voice shook. "They got away?"

He paused, considering. "I believe so. They reached their vessel before I was ordered to intercept. I refused. I let them live."

Relief hit me like a wave, quickly followed by something else. If others had escaped... maybe there was hope. Maybe someone was looking for me. Maybe this wasn't the end.

I forced my breathing to steady, though my heart wouldn't slow.

I turned my attention back to Tyvaron. "You said the game makers... they're still controlling others like you. Still running these games. Can you tell me what this is all about?"

His voice lowered. "Entertainment. It is all about entertainment. The game makers send people to this planet. Some are warriors, most are not. They are prey for the monsters. Monsters like me. They use us to hunt. Everything is filmed and broadcast across the galaxy. Death is what they want. So much death."

My stomach twisted at the word *prey*. That had been me. I had been dropped into this place like a piece of meat tossed into a pit, waiting for monsters like him to chase me down. But instead of killing me, he had... chosen me.

I shivered at the memory of that camera drone.

They had been *watching* me. Waiting for me to die for their entertainment. I felt sick at the thought.

"You saved me," I said eventually. "You could have followed your orders. But you didn't."

His eyes locked onto mine. "I could not."

A strange heat coiled in my chest, making it hard to breathe. Not fear. Not anymore. Something far more complicated.

The little dragon – *Ruby* – chirped softly beside me, pressing her warm body against my hip as if sensing my racing emotions.

I glanced down at her, stroking her head absently. She purred, smoke curling lazily from her tiny nostrils.

"So much has happened," I whispered. "I don't even know how to process any of this. And I've only been here for what, two days? You've been through so much more, Tyvaron."

He exhaled a deep breath, the faint metallic whirr beneath his skin softening. "You saved me too, Hazel."

I blinked at him, caught off guard. "Me?"

"You freed my mind." His voice was quiet now, almost reverent. "You broke the collar. You gave me reason to fight the chains."

I swallowed, my throat suddenly tight. "I just... I couldn't watch you suffer."

The silence that followed wasn't heavy. It was warm. Strange. Intimate.

I felt his gaze settle on me like a weight, but not one I wanted to escape from.

His voice rumbled again. Softer. Rougher.

"I owe you everything."

I held his gaze, feeling a strange heat rise to my cheeks. "Then I guess we're even. You didn't eat me."

His massive chest shook once. A low, almost amused rumble.

"No," he said. "Never you."

His words made warmth spread through my chest. I forced myself to focus.

There would be time later to process everything else. For now, Tyvaron was still hurt. No amount of regained memories or freedom from his collar would heal torn wings and open wounds.

I glanced at his side, where deep gashes still oozed faint streaks of blood. The membrane of his damaged wing trembled faintly with every breath. His body looked like it was holding together on sheer willpower alone.

"You need help," I said softly.

He shifted his weight slightly, exhaling a slow breath. "I am stronger now. But not whole."

"Your wounds will get worse if we don't do something." I glanced at the chii – and realised they had disappeared. "Where did they go? The chii? Could they help you? Heal you?"

"The chii have great wisdom. They restore minds. But bodies..." He paused. "They heal differently than us. They cannot repair what is broken inside me."

My heart sank. "Then what do we do?"

He was silent for a long moment, as though weighing every word.

"There is a place," he said finally. "A facility. The one where I was created. It holds machines, knowledge... things they used to change me." His voice tightened, bitter. "There are tools there that may allow me to repair what has been damaged. Become myself again. Turn from monster into...what I was before. If I can reach it."

I swallowed. "Where is it?"

"Far," he rasped. "High in the diamond mountains. Hidden. Guarded." His wings twitched again. "And dangerous."

Of course it was.

"Then we need to leave," I said, lifting my chin despite the fear curling in my stomach. "The longer we stay here, the worse your injuries will get."

Tyvaron's gaze settled on me. Warm. Steady. "You would come with me."

It wasn't a question. More a quiet statement of wonder.

I met his gaze, my voice small but firm. "Yes."

His chest rumbled again. And this time, it almost sounded like a purr. "I would like that. But I cannot allow it. They no longer use this place to create creatures like me, but there will still be guards. I cannot risk your safety. You are too precious to me."

I blinked, my heart skipping a beat at his words. *Precious.*

The word settled deep inside me, heating my chest in ways I wasn't prepared to deal with.

"Tyvaron," I said softly, forcing myself to focus, "I

understand that you want to protect me. I really do. But think about it. That other woman you saw – she was with the serpent, right? She wasn't hiding somewhere safe while he faced the danger alone. She was right there beside him."

He was silent, golden eyes watching me closely.

I took a slow breath and continued. "She didn't stay behind. She stayed with him. And they made it out together. You said it yourself – they're fighting the game makers. They are stronger together."

His head tilted slightly, as if turning this over in his mind.

"I might not be able to fight like you," I admitted. "But I can help. You won't have to watch your back. You won't have to face this alone." My voice grew firmer. "And I won't sit here doing nothing while you risk your life for me. "

His wings twitched. A low rumble vibrated through him, not angry. Something more like conflict.

"You are not weak," he said at last. "You have strength. But this path is dangerous, Hazel. The game makers will not allow me to reclaim what was stolen. They will fight to keep their weapon broken."

"Then let them try," I said, surprising myself with how steady my voice sounded. "I didn't survive this long to cower in a cave."

The little dragon chirped approvingly at my side, as if agreeing wholeheartedly with my reckless decision.

Tyvaron lowered his head until his snout was

almost level with my face. His breath was warm, his gaze intense.

"You are... extraordinary," he said softly.

I swallowed hard, my pulse quickening. "You've called me 'mine' since the moment you woke. So let me prove it."

His eyes narrowed slightly, as if searching for something in me. Testing my resolve.

Then, after a long, weighted pause, he nodded once.

"Together," he said.

"Together," I whispered.

I should have said no. I should have insisted she stay, where it was safe – if such a place even existed on Kalumbu. But the words had caught in my throat, strangled by something unfamiliar.

Hope.

Hazel, the tiny flame at the heart of all this chaos, had made a choice. Not because I asked. Not because I commanded. But because she *wanted* to.

That alone unravelled something in me.

She didn't understand what we would face. The climb would be hard, the storms fierce. The watchers might still patrol the skies. The facility – the place where they made me – was likely guarded by ancient machines and worse. Remnants of the experiments. Failures. Things not fit to survive, yet too useful to destroy.

I curled my tail beside me, careful not to let it brush

her by accident. Even now, every inch of me felt too sharp, too vast, too dangerous. But she was not afraid.

She stood with a slight groan, stretching her arms above her head. Was she injured? Was she in pain?

I scented the air for the smell of blood. There was none.

"Are you hurt?" I asked sharply.

"Just sore and bruised. Nothing, really. Should we go soon?"

I nodded, though my wings trembled with the effort.

"I need a little more time," I murmured. "My strength returns, but slowly. The damage runs deep. I am not able to fly yet. And you will have noticed that the only way out of this cave is to fly – at least for me. You might escape through the many tunnels, guided by the little one, but I would not be able to follow."

She nodded in return, crouching beside the little one who trilled sleepily in response.

The chii had gone as silently as they arrived. I could still feel the echo of their touch in my mind, like a gentle wind brushing through the ashes of something ancient. They had given me clarity. They had broken the chains around my mind and my memories, giving me freedom I'd thought lost forever. But I would have to fight for what came next on my own.

Hazel sat with her back against the stone wall, knees drawn to her chest. She watched the morning light creep slowly through the cave's wide mouth, filtering through mist and smoke.

"Tell me more about where we're going," she said eventually.

I took a breath.

"It is called Tel-Vhar, though I don't know what that name even means. It was hidden in the mountains long ago, shielded from both sky and sensors, built by people who came before us. Only the masters and their creations know how to find it."

"And you remember the way?"

"I will." I closed my eyes briefly. "Pieces are returning. Directions etched into bone. They left nothing to chance when they made us. In the beginning, they would summon us there regularly. For upgrades. For punishments. For experiments. But I have not been back in many planetary rotations. I half-wonder if they abandoned it when they focused more on the Trials rather than us abominations."

Her expression was unreadable. "And what happens if we get there... and it's not abandoned?"

I opened my eyes again. "Then I burn it to the ground."

She didn't flinch.

"I hope it won't come to that," she murmured. "But if it does... I'll be beside you."

The words hit me harder than I expected.

No one had stood beside me before.

Not since I lost myself.

Not until her.

I lowered my head, just enough to watch her from

the side, unsure what to do with the storm churning inside me. She was by my side. My ally. My...

I did not dare think that word.

I shifted my weight and winced. My wing ached where torn metal still fused imperfectly with bone. I would have to rest more before we could attempt the ascent.

"You will need protection," I said quietly. "Clothing. Supplies. The cold grows fierce the higher we climb."

She gave me a small, crooked smile. "If you haven't noticed, I don't exactly have a wardrobe right now."

My eyes swept over her body, seeing what I had tried to ignore. She was entirely naked, her pale scaleless skin so very soft and vulnerable, yet she held herself with confidence and determination. A flicker of possessiveness stirred inside me, primal and instinctive. She was so small. So without any means to protect herself. And yet she was not weak in the slightest.

I pulled my gaze away from her full breasts and the triangle of curls between her legs. I did not deserve to look there. I was not worthy of her beauty and strength.

I was a monster.

She was innocence and beauty and salvation.

"You will not go into the mountains like this," I rumbled. "I will find something. There are caves – near the edge of the forest – too small for me to enter, but the little one has scouted them for me. Old supplies were once stored there. Emergency packs, left by the masters. Perhaps they remain."

She nodded. "Good. Because I'm freezing, and I refuse to face evil lab scientists with my arse on display."

I didn't know what to say to that. So I let out a quiet huff, a sound she might one day recognize as laughter.

"How long until you can fly?" she asked, her voice softer now. Concern threaded through it like gold in stone.

"Tomorrow, maybe. Two days at most," I said. "I will need rest, food, and fire to speed my healing."

"And how exactly do you eat?"

I bared my teeth, amused by her wary glance.

"Not you," I promised.

"That's not what I asked."

"There are creatures in the lower valleys. Some small, some large. I can hunt when we leave the cave. Before, the little one will have to share its stores with me. It won't be more than a small snack for me, but hopefully, it will be enough."

"Can I help in any way?" she asked.

"Yes, you can. I need fire. I have enough in me to create sparks. The moss growing in these tunnels is flammable, when removed from the walls. If you are feeling up to it, you could gather some in a pile for me to set alight."

Hazel's breath caught slightly, and then she nodded again. "Alright. You rest, I'll see what I can find in the caves."

"Stay close," I warned, sharper than intended. "Those tunnels go deep. Not all of them are safe."

She gave me a look that might have melted stone. "I might be small, lizard boy, but I'm not stupid."

Lizard boy?

I blinked at her, unsure whether to growl or laugh.

She stood slowly, stretching again, and began walking towards one of the smaller tunnels, the little one bouncing after her with a joyful little puff of smoke. In her own language, I asked her to bring some of the meat she had stashed away in one of the caves. She had learned quickly that I had an appetite as large as my beastly form, so she kept her own food where I could not reach it.

I watched them go, the scent of her lingering like sunlight in the back of my throat.

She would go with me. Even into the place where my nightmares were born.

That meant more than I could put into words.

***

The two females returned just when I had finished drinking my fill from the cave's natural spring.

Hazel emerged from the tunnel with a determined expression and a bundle of moss in her arms, her skin covered in fine cave dust and her hair damp with exertion. The little one flapped behind her with a victorious chirp, clutching a stack of dried meat in her tiny claws.

It wouldn't even be enough for one proper bite.

"Is this enough?" Hazel asked, dropping the moss onto the stone with a grunt. "It was all I could carry."

"It is perfect," I said. My voice came out softer than I intended. "Thank you."

She gave me a wary glance, then her mouth curved into a tired smile. "You're welcome."

I shifted, stretching out one foreleg and opening my palm. A low rumble built in my chest as I summoned a controlled pulse of heat. The fire was weak inside me. I had used up most of it in the attack and with every rotation that passed, it took longer for my fire to restore itself. Maybe it had something to do with not having been summoned to Tel-Vhar in a long time.

A few sparks burst from my mouth, catching the dried moss instantly. It flared with a warm orange glow and began to crackle.

Hazel stepped back, wide-eyed but not afraid.

I breathed slowly, fanning the fire until it caught fully, then turned to the little one. She proudly looked at her tiny pile of meat - likely from one of the horned grazers that roamed the lower slopes. I didn't have the heart to tell her that this was not enough for someone as large as me.

Hazel must have noticed my hesitation. "Do you want me to go back and get you more meat? I can carry more than Ruby."

"I..." I hated to appear weak and needy in front of her, but without food, I would not be able to carry us to Tel-Vhar. "Yes. Please. If you can."

She grinned at me. "Yes, I can. And I will. You look hungry and I'd rather not become dragon breakfast."

Before I could reply, she hurried back into the tunnels, the little one following her with excited chirps. I wished I could follow. I wanted to be with her, every moment of every cycle. My heart burned to be close, feel her warmth, breathe in her scent. But I couldn't.

I shifted slightly, moving closer to the fire. The heat warmed my scales, travelling deep into my body where the embers were waiting to be reignited.

The warmth made me sleepy. I had almost flown over the fuzzy bridge into the land of dreams when the females returned. Hazel carried a huge pile of dried meat, while the little one had switched roles and held some more cave moss. I couldn't help but smile at the sight.

Hazel dropped the meat in front of me – the tiny stack that the little one had brought earlier had mysteriously disappeared in their absence – and I had to fight hard not to devour it all in one big bite.

But I was not the priority. She had not eaten anything since I had taken her to my cave. Hazel had to be starving.

"What does your kind eat?" I asked with genuine curiosity. "Do you like your meat raw?"

She snorted in amusement. "No. I mean, some people do like their steak bloody, but I'm a well-done sort of person. Honestly, I don't eat much meat, I try to stick to vegetarian food except when I really crave a burger or a doner kebab."

"Not all of these words make sense to me," I admitted. "This meat has been dried, but I will roast it for you if you wish."

I impaled several strips of meat on one of my claws and held them over the flames. My claws were not made for such a task, but I made them serve.

Hazel sat beside me, her knees pulled to her chest. The warmth of the fire painted her skin gold, and for a moment I forgot everything, including the pain.

The scent of roasting meat reminded me of my task. I turned my claws until the strips of meat were an even colour, before offering them to Hazel.

"I didn't know dragons could cook," she said with a smile. "I really appreciate you sharing your meal with me."

I let out a quiet huff. "We are full of surprises."

She glanced up at me, her expression unreadable. "You didn't have to do this."

"I know. I wanted to."

I watched her take a careful bite.

Her eyes widened.

"This is actually good."

I smiled again – a small thing, unfamiliar and strange on my draconic face. But I meant it.

"I will find you better food once I can hunt."

She chewed thoughtfully, then looked up. "You don't have to take care of me, you know."

"I want to."

Her breath caught. She didn't answer – but she didn't argue either.

I turned my gaze to the flames, letting the warmth

soak into the metal along my limbs, into the aching bones beneath my scales. There was still so much to heal. So much to face.

But for now, she was fed. She was safe.

And that was enough.

Tyvaron fell asleep after he'd eaten every tiny scrap of meat. I let him rest, watching his chest rise and fall. His breathing seemed to be deeper now, less of a struggle. At some point, I got some more moss and cleaned his wounds again. He didn't wake, which must have meant that I didn't cause him any further pain.

Once I had thrown the bloodstained moss out of the cave's gaping entrance, I curled up in front of him. Ruby immediately appeared at my side, chittering happily. Tiny tendrils of smoke came from her nostrils. She was just too cute to be real.

And she had no shame whatsoever. She snuggled against Tyvaron, rubbing her scales against his with glee, before her eyes fell shut. A tiny snore escaped her open mouth.

I swallowed a chuckle, not wanting to wake her.

If she did it, why shouldn't I? I was cold – the fire

was quickly growing smaller – and he was asleep. He wouldn't notice.

I slowly inched closer, until my back pressed against his scales. The warmth of his scales seeped into my skin, comforting in a way that made no sense. He was a dragon. A cyborg weapon. An alien. And yet... I felt safer here than I ever had in my old bed back home.

Just for a minute, I let myself rest.

The fire crackled softly beside us. Ruby let out another snore, twitching slightly in her sleep, her tiny claws curling against Tyvaron's foreleg.

My eyes drifted shut.

I didn't mean to fall asleep. Just a few seconds, I told myself. A moment to breathe.

But my body had other plans.

Wrapped in warmth, surrounded by smoke and stone and dragons, I let the exhaustion take me.

For once, there were no nightmares.

Only stillness.

Only quiet.

Only peace.

I woke to a strange silence.

No smoke, no soft snores, no distant dragon breath. Just the quiet hush of morning in a cave that felt suddenly... empty.

I sat up with a start.

Ruby was gone. Tyvaron, too.

Panic flared for a heartbeat – until a soft gust of wind curled through the mouth of the cave, bringing with it a warm scent I was beginning to associate with him. Fire, metal, sky. And something... earthy. Real.

Then a shadow shifted in the entrance.

Tyvaron stepped inside, wings tucked, claws surprisingly silent against the stone. His body moved with more strength than the day before. Not fully healed, but stronger. Steadier.

He was carrying something in his arms – no, *someone*.

Ruby.

The tiny dragonlet dangled like a satisfied kitten, belly round and eyes bright.

"She found fruit," Tyvaron said, his deep voice rumbling softly. "Then fell into a bush and refused to come out. I had to negotiate."

I stared at him. Then at Ruby, who blinked innocently and puffed smoke in my direction.

"Negotiate?" I echoed, lips twitching.

"She made demands. I made counter-offers."

I laughed. It felt good to laugh. A little too good. Something about seeing this enormous, terrifying creature talking about bartering with a baby dragon over berries made the world tilt a bit more in my favour.

Tyvaron set Ruby down. She waddled over and pressed her head into my side like she'd been gone for years instead of minutes.

"I would have brought you food, but I had to carry her. She ate too much and couldn't fly. Silly little one."

He looked at the tiny dragon with nothing but love.

"We can stop there again on the way to the supply caves. Then we'll try and find you some clothes, rations, maybe a weapon if we're lucky. Your species is not equipped very well."

I crossed my arms and glared at him. "My species is harder than you think."

"I'm coming to realise that." He flashed me a toothy grin. "I'm ready."

I blinked up at him.

His scales gleamed in the morning light – shimmering turquoise and aquamarine, the mother-of-pearl sheen more alive than ever. His wings were still ragged at the edges, but they held their shape. I couldn't see any fresh blood. His limbs were steady. His eyes? Focused. Clear.

"You're sure?" I asked quietly.

"I can carry us both. Slowly, and only for short stretches. We will travel by wing and by foot. It will not be easy." He tilted his head slightly. "You can still choose to stay."

I stood and brushed cave dust from my thighs. "And miss out on the chance to storm an evil lab on the back of a cyborg dragon? Not a chance."

He huffed. "You're mad."

"You're only now noticing?"

Tyvaron crouched low, letting me climb onto his back between the plates of heavier scales. His skin was warm beneath me, familiar now. My fingers curled around the natural ridges near his neck.

"Ruby will follow us," he said, and I realised she'd fallen asleep in a corner. Food coma. "She knows the way to the caves. And even if we've moved on by then, she can follow my scent."

The wind hit as soon as we stepped from the cave. The cliff dropped away below us, a breathtaking view of golden trees and red-rock ridges stretching for miles. In the distance, the diamond mountains I had travelled towards a lifetime ago. Somewhere out there, danger waited.

So did answers. And more.

"Ready?" Tyvaron asked.

I looked down at the sheer drop and regretted it instantly. I focused instead on the clouds above, the golden sun.

"Yes. Let's do this."

He leapt.

The wind swallowed us whole.

And the journey began.

***

Flying wasn't what I expected.

It wasn't graceful, or peaceful, or magical.

It was *terrifying*.

Wind howled in my ears. My eyes watered instantly. Every instinct screamed that we were too high, that I wasn't meant to be here, clinging to the back of a biomechanical dragon as he soared over cliffs like gravity was a suggestion and death a dare.

My arms ached from gripping the thick ridge at the base of his neck. The motion of his wings threw my body back and forth like a sack of laundry in a storm. I pressed my chest to his back, trying to stay low, trying not to think about how very far the ground was below us.

And yet...

The view was unlike anything I'd ever seen.

Beneath us stretched endless forests in shades of fire interrupted only by pale rock spires that jutted up like broken bones. In the far distance, the Diamond Mountains glinted like frost-tipped teeth. A storm brewed on the horizon, purple clouds flashing with flickers of lightning, but the skies above us were clear.

And Tyvaron's body, beneath me, was solid and warm.

I trusted him.

That fact hit me like a second wave of vertigo.

I trusted this giant alien weapon of destruction. Because he'd brought me food. Because he'd cooked for me. Because he'd let me sleep against him and hadn't tried to bite my head off.

It wasn't *rational*. But it was real.

He banked gently to the left, gliding lower, and shouted something over the wind. I couldn't make out the words, but I caught the intent: *Hold on tight*.

I did.

We descended sharply, my stomach dropping as wind roared around us. Below, a jagged ravine opened into a narrow ledge flanked by two crumbling stone pillars. It didn't look like much from the air, but as we neared, I saw the outline of a cave mouth – half-collapsed, hidden by vines.

Tyvaron landed hard enough to drive the breath from my lungs. His wings flared wide to slow the impact, claws scraping against the stone as he skidded forward and came to a stop with a low grunt.

I slid off him the moment he crouched low enough.

My knees shook and my legs felt like jelly.

"Ten out of ten for drama," I huffed. "Zero for comfort."

He made a rumbling noise that I *thought* might be a laugh. "With the state of my wings, I would have preferred to walk, too. But this was quicker."

"No kidding."

I glanced around. The air was cooler here, shaded by rock and heavy foliage. The cave mouth yawned ahead of us, partially filled by fallen rocks, but still passable. Pale moss clung to the walls, and something that looked like frost shimmered faintly in the deeper shadows.

"This is it?" I asked.

He nodded. "One of the smaller cache sites. I found it cycles ago. Couldn't enter myself. Sent the little one instead. She told me what was inside."

"And you trust her?"

"With my life," he said simply.

That shut me up.

Together, we approached the entrance. I ducked low to avoid a hanging root – bright orange like most of the trees here - and squeezed through the narrow gap in the rock. The air inside was cooler still, tinged with dust and something faintly metallic. My bare feet slipped on smooth stone, and I had to use the wall to steady myself. I really hoped they had shoes stashed in here.

The sunlight was blocked behind me as Tyvaron tried to peek inside. He couldn't follow, but his voice rumbled close.

"I will remain here. If anything moves, shout for help."

"Comforting," I muttered under my breath, and pressed deeper inside.

It was only a short tunnel, maybe ten or fifteen meters, before it opened into a chamber about the size of a small house. There was no glowing moss like in Tyvaron's cave. I squeezed my eyes together, trying to make out what the shapes inside the cave were hiding. Hopefully not a sleeping beast.

A large cube to my right caught my eye. Metal glinted in the dim light as I approached cautiously. A crate of some sort.

And in it – bingo.

Supplies.

If there had ever been a system to the crate's contents, it had all long ago jumbled together. In the end, I grabbed as much as I could and carried it outside into the sunshine.

"I see you were successful," Tyvaron said appreciatively.

"That is yet to be seen. I just brought everything. No idea if any of it is helpful."

I searched through the pile, discarding empty containers and plastic bags that may have once held food. Most of it was broken, rubbish or I didn't know what purpose it could serve, but amongst the rubbish were a few gems.

A blanket that I could wrap around me like a skirt. A sleeveless shirt made for someone much bigger with four armholes instead of the usual two. A shoulder bag made from a crinkly sort of material that shimmered brightly in the sun. And best of all, a knife, the blade still sharp.

No shoes, but I cut two strips off the blanket and wrapped them around my feet. Better than nothing.

I put on my new outfit, glad there was no mirror. I had to look ridiculous. But still – it was a huge improvement on walking around naked.

I turned to Tyvaron and spread my arms, laughing to cover my awkwardness.

"Ta-daaaa! How do I look?"

He didn't speak.

His gaze swept over me from head to toe. Not with hunger, not with judgment. Just... appreciation. Soft, warm, full of something I didn't dare name.

"You look prepared," he said at last.

"I feel it," I replied, and I meant it. "Next stop: food. And then the evil lab of doom."

He huffed again, his eyes glittering. "I saw some berries over there. And see those gnarly trees over there? They harbour large nuts, a bit oily but I have seen other beings eat them. I shall rattle the closest tree and you can tell me if they're any good."

Off he walked, limping slightly, while I watched with a smile curving my lips. He was providing me with food again. I could get used to this.

Just when Hazel dropped the last half-eaten nut, declaring that she was unable to eat even one more mouthful, the little one's wingbeats sounded behind me.

Ruby landed on a boulder with a chirp and shook herself proudly, as if announcing her return to duty.

"We're ready," Hazel said, brushing her hands together and slinging the shimmering bag over her shoulder. "Or at least, as ready as we'll ever be."

I studied her for a long moment.

She looked absurd. The shirt gaped at the shoulders, the makeshift skirt barely stayed up, and her feet were bound in fabric that would offer little protection in the climb ahead. And yet she carried herself like a warrior.

No fear in her stance. No hesitation in her voice.

I bowed my head slightly. "Climb on."

She did, with practiced ease now, settling into

place between the armoured ridges of my back. Ruby leapt into the air and circled once overhead, then veered north. Towards the mountains. Towards Tel-Vhar.

We followed.

The journey was slow.

My wings could not carry us far before pain forced us to land. We travelled by foot where we could, scaling narrow trails and crossing ridgelines that crumbled beneath our weight.

Correction: *my* weight.

The sky above turned colder with every hour. The wind sharpened, tasting of ice and oncoming storms. Clouds gathered thick and low, pressing down on the mountains like a warning.

Hazel spoke little, conserving her strength. But when she did speak, it always pierced deeper than she knew.

"Do you think we'll find answers there?"

"I think we'll find ghosts," I replied.

She fell silent after that.

By the third short flight to carry us up an unscalable ledge, I could see the facility in the distance – a black scar on the mountain's face, half-buried in rock. Its shape had changed since I last saw it, but the signature was the same. My body remembered. My mind recoiled.

I'd told myself I was ready.

I lied.

Hazel shifted behind me, sensing my tension. Her

hand rested lightly on the back of my neck. She didn't speak. She didn't have to.

Her presence calmed me more than I cared to admit.

We rounded the final ridge. My entire body was aching. One gash at the top of my wing had re-opened, oozing hot blood. I wouldn't be much use in a fight, should the lab still be guarded.

And then I felt it.

The air thickened. The wind shifted.

And then the sky screamed.

A shadow tore across the clouds, followed by a roar that made the very stones beneath our feet vibrate. I turned sharply, wings spreading to shield Hazel as a tyvarin descended from the heavens like a falling star.

Almost my size. Sleeker. Metallic. Vicious.

His scales were obsidian black with streaks of molten silver, and his eyes glowed crimson.

He was still trapped, forced to do the masters' bidding. He had no awareness.

Still theirs.

I shuddered at the thought that not long ago, this had been me. A mindless monster, created to kill without morals, without thought.

Hazel gasped behind me. "Is that...?"

"A tyvarin," I growled. "One of my kin."

I knew him, had flown by his side, fought next to him, but I did not know his name. I was the only one who had been given a formal name by the masters. Tyvaron, leader of the tyvarin.

But he no longer recognised me as such. My collar was broken and with it, any control I may have had over the others.

He slammed into the earth just ahead of us, claws carving trenches into the rock. His neck arched like a striking serpent, lips peeling back to reveal rows of jagged teeth. His collar – intact and humming with brutal energy – flared with light.

The sound he made was not language. Not a voice.

It was a command scream. An execution protocol.

I stepped forward, placing myself between Hazel and the other dragon.

"You won't have her," I said, voice low, deadly. "Not today."

The enemy tyvarin didn't speak. And I realised he wasn't interested in her.

He wanted to destroy me.

And I wasn't strong enough to fight. He was at the top of his strength, I was injured and exhausted. And I had to protect Hazel.

But that was something he did not have. Someone to fight for. A reason to live.

He charged.

I moved fast – faster than my injuries allowed. My wings snapped wide, flaring to full span in a defensive arc as I stepped forward, putting my body between Hazel and the oncoming monster. Pain lanced through my side. I forced it down. I couldn't fly. Not in this condition. Not while she was so close. And if he reached her – if he touched her –

He would not.

Not while I still breathed.

I met his charge head-on.

There was no time to think, no time to calculate. My muscles screamed, my wing burned, but I launched myself forward, claws outstretched. We collided like meteors, the impact shaking the mountainside. Stone shattered beneath our feet. His teeth snapped inches from my throat.

I twisted, raking my claws down his shoulder. Sparks flew where metal met metal. He shrieked – no pain, only fury – then slammed his bulk against mine, driving me back. My injured wing collapsed beneath the pressure. Agony ripped through me.

But I did not fall.

Hazel was behind me. I would not fall.

He lashed out with his tail – razor-barbed and seething with kinetic charge. I ducked under it, using his momentum against him, shoving him sideways into a boulder that split with the force of the impact. Dust and debris exploded into the air.

His collar pulsed again – bright red, violent. A jolt of command struck the space between us like lightning. I felt it even from here, the echo of what once held me, the command to *kill*.

He lunged again.

This time, I sidestepped. Not out of weakness – out of control. I'd learned from my pain. I would not be their puppet anymore.

He was faster. Stronger.

But I was free.

He didn't understand what that meant. He couldn't. And that gave me the only edge I had left.

"Hear me," I roared as he turned, "you don't have to obey!"

He didn't slow. Of course he didn't.

But maybe, just maybe, a fragment of him still listened.

I'd bought a heartbeat of space. Enough to glance back, to be sure Hazel hadn't moved. She stood behind a rise, eyes wide, hands clenched in determination – not fear.

She trusted me.

And I would not let her down.

Claws met claws.

The impact cracked the stone beneath us. My limbs buckled, but I held my ground. The other tyvarin snarled – a mechanical sound, all static and rage – and slashed at my side. Sparks flew where metal met metal. My shoulder burned. I drove forward, slamming him with the full weight of my body.

He didn't even flinch.

He was faster. Stronger. His mind was gone, but his body was perfect.

He ducked low and struck again – a savage blow to my ribs that sent me skidding backward, gouging deep lines in the rock. I bared my teeth, growling through the fire that bloomed inside me. Hazel scrambled behind a boulder, calling my name, but I couldn't look at her. Couldn't risk dividing my attention for even a breath.

He lunged.

I twisted.

Too slow.

His claws raked across my flank, peeling scales like bark. I roared, flame flickering from my jaws, but I held it back. If Hazel was anywhere near the blast radius...

No. I wouldn't risk it.

Another strike.

This one hit my chest, near the collar's former anchoring point. Pain lanced through my core, old circuits still twitching in memory of obedience. I stumbled, one knee cracking against stone.

He reared back, preparing to finish it.

And that's when I saw it.

The collar.

It sparked, flaring with every movement, every strike. Pulsing commands. I recognised the rhythm – the chain of programming woven through every strike.

Kill the traitor.

Kill the broken one.

I wasn't just an enemy.

I was an infection.

A warning to the others.

I was proof that control could be broken – and that made me dangerous.

He roared again, lifting off the ground for a final strike from above.

I planted all four limbs, ready to die standing.

But then I heard a sound – a cry – behind me.

Hazel.

No.

She stepped into the open. Her voice rang out like a blade. "Tyvaron!"

The enemy dragon hesitated, just for a breath.

But it was enough.

I turned, gathered every last shred of fire left in me, and aimed not at his body – but at the collar.

A precise, narrow beam of heat.

It struck.

The collar ignited.

Sparks exploded around his neck. The dragon screamed, but it wasn't rage this time. It was pain. Confusion.

His wings flared wide as he reeled backward, crashing against a stone outcrop and leaving deep gouges in the rock.

I staggered forward, trying to reach him, to end it before he could recover.

But he didn't attack.

He trembled.

Smoke poured from the broken collar. The crimson glow in his eyes flickered. Died.

He sagged to his knees, massive chest heaving.

For a moment, I thought it was over.

Then he lifted his head – and I saw his eyes.

They were no longer red.

Just empty.

Like something vital had been torn away.

He collapsed.

Dust rose around him.

And silence fell.

I didn't move. Couldn't move. My limbs shook. My vision swam. This fight had taken everything out of me. But it had been worth it. Hazel was alive. So was the little one, still hiding behind a boulder.

Hazel's footsteps reached me moments later, her hands warm where they touched my shoulder.

"Tyvaron," she whispered. "Are you okay?"

I blinked slowly, lowering my head to hers.

"I will be."

We both looked at the fallen tyvarin. Still breathing, but barely. A broken shell.

"Can he be saved?" she asked.

I didn't answer right away.

I didn't know. Didn't have any experience with this.

It hadn't been just the removal of the collar that had saved me. It had been Hazel, her presence, her light. She had saved me.

This tyvarin didn't have that. I couldn't provide him with a female to care for, to fall for.

Wait.

I was not falling for her.

I was not.

I was.

A moment ago, the world had narrowed to smoke and sound and the echo of Tyvaron's roars.

Now it was quiet.

Too quiet.

The obsidian-scaled dragon lay slumped against the ridge, his chest rising and falling in shallow, shuddering breaths. He was alive. Barely. Tyvaron hadn't killed him, though he easily could have. Instead, he had knocked him out with the kind of brutal precision that came from knowing every weak point in a body like his own.

He stood over the fallen tyvarin now, blood dripping from a fresh gash in his shoulder, wings trembling with exhaustion. His own wounds had reopened, staining the rocky slope with streaks of crimson and silver.

There was no way he'd be able to fly any further.

I wanted to run to him, to wrap my arms around

that giant, wounded frame and hold him together with sheer willpower.

Instead, I stepped quietly to his side and laid a hand on his foreleg.

He didn't say anything right away. Just stared at the fallen dragon. When he finally spoke, his voice was raw.

"He's like I was. Lost. Bound. I wanted to save him."

"We will," I said. "But you can't help him if you bleed out on this mountainside. Let's get inside the lab."

He finally tore his gaze away, nodding once. "We leave him here for now. Later, we shall return. Help however we can. And if we cannot... I will give him a merciful death."

I shuddered at the determination in his voice. He would do it, no doubt about it. But I was glad he was going to look for a different solution first.

We didn't speak again for a while.

Tyvaron walked slowly beside me, his breathing laboured, each step leaving a smear of blood on the stone. His wing dragged behind him, limp and broken, but he kept moving. He didn't ask for help. Didn't complain. Just pressed on, one massive claw after the next.

I stayed close. Not because I thought he'd fall, but because I needed to. Because if he stumbled, I'd be there. Even if I couldn't catch him, at least I'd be by his side.

It was a silly notion. The likelihood was I'd be turned into Hazel-mousse by his weight. But that did not make me put any distance between us.

The path narrowed ahead, funnelling into a steep channel of carved stone leading directly to the dark scar in the cliffside – the lab. Tel-Vhar. The place that had turned Tyvaron from man into monster.

The closer we came, the more the air changed. Colder. Sharper. Tainted with ozone and something almost metallic. Not quite blood, but not far off. My skin prickled with it. My stomach tightened.

Tyvaron growled something to Ruby. Dragon language. Ruby fluttered her wings, chirped excitedly, then flew off, darting from rock to rock, then vanishing entirely when the cliff face swallowed her shadow. I craned my neck, trying to follow her movements, but she was already gone.

"What is she doing?" I asked, my heavy breathing disrupting the words.

"There are drones. Watchers. Automated sentries built to kill anything not coded to the masters' control." His voice dropped to a growl. "They will follow heat. Movement. Sound."

"So... Ruby's basically bait?"

His silence confirmed it.

"She's quick. Clever," Tyvaron rasped after a while, as if to reassure himself. "And they won't see her coming."

I didn't like it. But I trusted her. She wasn't just a baby. She'd survived here longer than I had. And Tyvaron believed in her. That was enough.

We waited behind a jagged outcrop near the entry point. The black mouth of the lab loomed just a hundred meters ahead. There was no movement, no sign of life.

Then, somewhere up the slope, a shrill chirp rang out.

Followed by a second.

Then a blur of movement – pale purple and smoke trailing behind – shot out across the clearing ahead.

Three metallic forms detached from the stone like shadows peeling loose. Sleek. Spiderlike. They scuttled after her in perfect synchronisation, lasers pulsing from their underbellies as they vanished into the ravine.

Creepy as fuck.

The red light flickered. Paused. Then stilled.

Tyvaron turned to me. "Now."

We moved fast, or as fast as an injured dragon and an out-of-shape human without shoes could. The gates before us groaned, ancient and rusted, and slid open just enough for us to squeeze through.

A small squeeze for humanity, a big squeeze for dragonkind. But this facility had been built for the tyvarin. The gate was just about large enough to accommodate Tyvaron.

Inside, the light changed. Cold. Fluorescent.

A corridor stretched before us – wide enough for Tyvaron, though barely – lined with dark metal and strange symbols carved into the walls. The air was sterile. Still. The scent of dust and decay sat heavy in my nose.

Every step echoed against the metal walls, a cold hum of distant power vibrating beneath my feet. Light strips flickered overhead, some still functional, others sputtering like dying stars. The entire place felt... wrong. Like it was waiting for us.

Tyvaron moved slowly beside me, quiet now, his breathing steady but tense. His claws clicked against the smooth floor, leaving faint smudges of blood in our wake. The deeper we went, the more the air thickened. Metallic. Sterile. And under it all – something else. Decay.

We passed the first room without speaking.

A long window gave us a view inside. At first, I thought it was empty – just machinery and broken glass – but then I saw the shape on the table. Or what was left of it.

A massive, twisted ribcage. Hollow. Cracked. Half-buried under surgical tools the size of scythes. Dark stains marked the floor beneath it.

I gagged.

Tyvaron's growl vibrated through the walls. Not directed at me. At the memory. At the horror.

"They dissected one of us here," he said, voice hoarse.

"One of the... tyvarin?"

He nodded once. "A failure, maybe. Or a rebel. Or just a test subject." He didn't say more.

We moved on.

The second chamber was worse.

Glass pods lined the walls, most shattered. Inside the ones that still stood, floating in pale fluid, were fragments – claws, limbs, twisted remains of what might once have been wings. One still had an eye floating inside. It blinked.

I stumbled back, bile rising in my throat.

"What the hell is this place?" I whispered.

Tyvaron didn't answer. He didn't need to.

This was where he'd been turned into a weapon. And others like him hadn't survived the process.

We passed sealed doors with claw marks on the inside. Rusted restraints. Broken restraints. Control panels that still sparked when we brushed too close. I didn't want to know what had been behind some of those doors. Tyvaron never looked away. He knew every room. Every shadow.

He hesitated just before a door, slightly ajar, as if someone had forgotten to close it. I could see it in every line of his body – the memories clawing back. Pain. Fire. Screams.

I reached up, laid a hand gently on his side.

"I'm with you," I whispered.

And together, we stepped into the place where his nightmares began.

The air here was colder. The lights steadier. And in the centre of the room stood something that looked part shrine, part machine.

A circular platform, raised slightly off the ground,

with metallic limbs arched overhead like claws ready to descend. Coils lined the base, and a strange shimmer danced in the air above it – like heatwaves without heat. The air hummed with energy.

"This is it," Tyvaron said quietly.

I turned to him. He was still bleeding. Still shaking. And yet his eyes were clearer than I'd ever seen them.

"This will help you heal?" I asked. My voice shook slightly.

"In a way."

"And it still works?"

He tapped a screen with one of his claws and it flickered to life, showing symbols and writing I could not read.

"I believe so." He sounded tense, so very tense. I wanted to hug him, tell him everything was going to be alright – but was it? Really?

I tried to stay rational, focusing on what was in front of me rather than what could happen. "You've seen it used before?"

"Yes," he rasped. "Once. Long ago. They forced one of us – one who'd clung to his mind – to shift back into his original form. It worked. Briefly. They recorded everything. Then they... took him apart."

My blood turned to ice. "And you want to try it?"

"I have to." He looked at me, golden eyes burning. "My memories are here. My name. My true form. Everything they stripped away might still exist inside this place. I can feel it. The chii woke me... but this could return what they stole."

I stepped forward, putting a hand on his foreleg. "Are you sure?"

He hesitated. Then nodded.

I let my hand linger just a second longer. Then I stepped back.

Tyvaron limped towards the platform. Each step left a smear of blood, a mark of everything he'd endured. He climbed onto it, claws folding close to his body, wings drooping low.

The machine began to hum.

"You will have to press that button," he said quietly, pointing at a green console with his least injured claw.

I took a deep breath. Was I really going to do this? What if it killed him? What if I'd been the one to start the machine that would take his life? Could I live with that?

But there was no alternative. He wanted this. I had to trust him.

Lights sparked overhead. The shimmer intensified. The air grew sharp, electric.

He looked at me one last time. "If I do not return…"

"You will," I said, firm.

He nodded once – and closed his eyes.

And then the machine came to life.

TYVARON

I flew.

The wind rushed beneath my wings, cold and bright and wild.

I soared.

No pain. No weight. No metal embedded in bone.

Just me – skin and scale, muscle and memory – riding the thermals like I was born to touch the stars. The sun burned golden above the peaks of Valhyr's Crown, catching the shimmer of my aquamarine scales with every beat of my wings. Below, waterfalls carved through black stone. Trees swayed in radiant hues – crimson, emerald, violet. My people called this place *Vareth-kai*, the breath between worlds. Sacred skies. My skies.

Home.

I laughed.

The sound broke free before I could stop it – joy,

uncontained and irreverent, echoing over the cliffs. My horns were caressed by the wind as I spun into a steep dive, tail slicing the air behind me, my arms flaring for balance. I wasn't alone – others flew with me. Friends. Kin. Winged forms dancing in synchrony, their laughter rising like birdsong.

We were fast. Strong. Alive.

Free.

Someone called my name. A voice like chimes in wind. Familiar. Loved.

But the memory blurred.

The light changed.

Pain.

A spear of sound shattered the air. Not a weapon. A trap. Something deeper. A frequency that sliced through bone and thought. Wings crumpled mid-flight. My body dropped like stone, crashing through trees, through light, through memory.

When I opened my eyes again, I was in darkness.

Bound.

Burning.

Everything that came after was steel and screaming. Agony and blades. Collars that made thinking hurt and obedience feel like blessed silence. They changed my shape, piece by piece. Fused metal into flesh. Made me forget my name. My skies. My people.

But not that flight.

Not that moment of perfect freedom.

I remembered it now.

And I would take it back.

———

Pain.

Not the ripping, burning agony I remembered from the experiments – but something deeper. Like being pulled apart and stitched together all at once. A shattering. A rebirth.

I passed out. Awoke. Passed out again. Woke to yet more pain.

Then silence.

I opened my eyes.

The platform was beneath me, the cold of the metal pressing against unfamiliar skin. Smaller. Softer. And yet... still mine.

My hands – hands – rested on either side of me, claw-tipped fingers curling slowly. My tail lay coiled against the platform, thick and muscular, but shorter now. My wings flexed behind me, their span reduced but functional, the membrane intact. I could not feel any injuries, no more blood seeping from gaping wounds. I had been healed.

I still had scales. Glimmering hues of aquamarine and dark turquoise shimmered across my body. My chest and shoulders remained plated in thicker, armour-like scales. But my shape... it was *me* again. Upright. Balanced.

Bipedal.

I sat up slowly, blinking as the world swayed.

My vision adjusted quickly – too quickly for an organic being. The implant systems remained. My metal enhancements had been… compressed, somehow. No longer overtly visible, but I could feel them beneath the surface. The fire, too. Folded away, like coiled serpents beneath skin.

A hiss escaped my throat.

Not in pain.

In wonder.

The machine had worked.

"Tyvaron?" Hazel's voice – soft, uncertain – cut through the fog. I turned.

She stood a few steps away, her eyes wide, lips parted.

"H–Hazel," I said.

It came out rough. Too low. I coughed. My vocal cords were still recalibrating. But the word had been mine.

Hazel blinked, stepping forward like she wasn't sure if I was real.

"You did it," she whispered. "You're – "

She stopped. Her gaze roamed across my body, lingering on my face, my chest, the curve of my wings. I didn't think I looked like I used to – whatever that meant. My body didn't quite feel like it did in my memories. But I looked like someone.

Someone she could talk to. Touch. Choose.

Someone closer to her size.

"I remember more," I said, voice steadier. "Fragments. My name… it's close. I can feel it."

She reached out slowly. "Can I...?"

I gave a single nod.

Her fingers brushed my cheek.

"I think I can still become Tyvaron again," I said, catching her gaze again. "This form – it's not a replacement. It's encoded. Quantum-compressed."

Hazel tilted her head. "Like... folded space?"

"Yes. My dragon form exists in a separate compression field. I can access it. Shift at will. Like the tyvarin they first tried this technology on. Or at least... I think that's what's happening. I will have to try it. But not for a while. Not for a very long time."

"So... you can be both." Her fingers brushed my cheek – slow, tentative. Testing if I was real.

"You're warm," she whispered.

"I still have blood," I said softly. "Still breathe. I'm just less likely to roast you alive with my fire breath."

She didn't smile. Not yet. Her gaze roamed over my face like she was trying to connect this version of me with the dragon she'd slept beside. Her fingers lingered for a moment longer than they needed to, then drifted down to hover near my collarbone – near the place where scales shimmered softly under my skin.

"So this is you," she said at last. "The real you."

I shook my head. "It's part of me. One shape of many. But I... feel closer to who I was." I met her gaze, the fire behind her eyes stealing the breath from my lungs. "Because of you."

That caught her off guard. She blinked, her breath hitching.

"You're not just saying that because I cleaned your wounds and brought you moss for your fire, are you?"

"No," I said. "Though I'll admit, the moss helped."

She laughed then – short, breathless, a little too quick. And I saw it: the flush rising in her cheeks. The way her fingers curled slightly, like she didn't trust them not to touch me again.

I stepped closer. Just enough to feel the warmth of her. Not touching, but almost. My voice dropped low.

"I haven't been like this in a long time. I don't know what I'm doing."

"Me neither," she murmured. "But I keep... wanting to be closer. Even when it's terrifying."

I let my hand brush hers. Scaled knuckles against soft skin. Her fingers didn't pull away.

Her eyes met mine, wide and uncertain.

"If I stay too close," she said quietly, "I might forget how to leave."

"Then don't," I said.

We stood like that beneath the machine – not kissing, not touching any more than that faint brush of fingers – but it was enough. The air between us pulsed with something fierce and unspoken.

I didn't have a word for it.

But the shape of it was forming.

The machine powered down with a sharp hiss, making us break apart as if we'd been caught doing something forbidden.

I stood still on the platform, rolled my shoulders, shook my wings. My body felt strange yet also familiar.

I was lighter now – not in mass, but in mind. The cold metal that had once threaded through every nerve and thought no longer sang with commands. The collar was gone. And beneath the thickened armour of my hybrid form, I could feel the echo of what I had once been.

More than a tyvarin. More than a weapon.

My name was close, so very close. My memories were lingering behind a layer of fog, just out of reach, but I got enough glimpses to know that I had been part of a clan, a family. I had been loved. I'd had a good life, before I'd been taken from my world.

And maybe, just maybe, I could return to that world one day. Would Hazel join me? Meet my kind? She was from a different planet. I realised I didn't even know what species she was. She'd mentioned it, hoomin, something like that? But it didn't mean anything to me. And she likely wanted to return home to her people, if we found a way off Kalumbu.

But those were worries for later. For now, we had to get out of here before the guards returned.

I stepped off the platform, wobbling slightly. I wasn't used to walking on two legs anymore. My tail helped me balance my unfamiliar shape, but the wings dragged slightly.

Hazel moved to meet me, cautious, searching my face for something. Maybe for reassurance that I was still *me* – still the beast who had cooked her dinner and carried her through the skies. I was. And I wasn't. I wasn't sure how to explain that yet.

But her hand slipped into mine.

She said nothing. She didn't need to.

We left the room together.

Back through corridors that had once echoed with screams. Through the wreckage of the lab's dark history. But this time, I saw it with different eyes – not just the suffering inflicted here, but the systems. The network.

The possibilities.

"I wonder…" I said, stopping in front of a closed door that I recognised from my tyvarin memories. It was much smaller than the others and I wouldn't have been able to fit through it in my monster form.

Hazel looked at me quizzically. "Yes?"

"We should go in here. I want to check something."

I reached out, placing my clawed hand – now more hand than talon – against the door panel. A soft *click* answered.

It opened.

Inside was a narrow room filled with consoles and glowing interfaces. Long-dead screens sparked to life at our presence.

"What is this place?" Hazel asked, stepping in behind me.

"Control," I murmured. "I think this is where they sent orders to the collars. Where they managed the network that linked us all. I remember this place. I saw it once, long ago… I wasn't supposed to, but I got a glimpse of it. Enough to know that this room is important."

I crossed to the main console. Screens flickered,

displaying strings of data in the old language of the masters. I'd been under their control long enough to understand the basics.

Hazel hovered beside me. "Can you... turn it off? Free the other tyvarin?"

"I hope so. This is not the only place from which they can control us. They have a space station circling the planet, which is why this lab is now unoccupied. They don't need to be here to send commands to the collars. But this is the original control centre. If we're lucky, everything sent from here overrides commands from other sources."

My fingers danced across the screen – scales shifting slightly as I moved. I had to guess at some of the options, but I didn't get any error messages. I was amazed this system still worked this smoothly. Maybe it got updates sent remotely.

A schematic appeared. Red dots blinked across a map of Kalumbu. tyvarin. At least fifty of them. Maybe more, scattered through the mountains and forests. Sleeping. Waiting. Hunting.

Still enslaved.

And not as many as I remembered. Where were the others? Sent to other planets? Dead?

A cold shiver ran over my scales. My brothers.

I felt Hazel step closer, her breath warm against my arm. "Can you break the connection?"

I nodded once. "I can disable the signal that feeds their collars. Not destroy the collars – not from here.

But cut them off from the masters' commands. Give them a chance to wake up. The way I did."

"And if they don't?"

"I don't know. Maybe they will retreat somewhere, waiting for new commands. They will not hunt. They will do nothing but wait. Until the masters repair what we break today."

I pressed my hand to the activation pad.

There was a pulse. A low, thrumming sound, like a heartbeat suddenly cut short.

The red dots vanished.

All of them.

Gone.

Hazel sucked in a breath. "You did it."

"I hope so," I whispered. "I hope they feel the silence now. I hope it gives them peace."

I didn't feel triumphant. Not yet. But I did feel... lighter.

A soft sound interrupted the stillness – a low, rumbling roar from far away.

The fallen tyvarin.

Hazel and I exchanged a look, then moved quickly through the corridor, retracing our path. The outer gate still stood open. The black-scaled tyvarin lay where I had left him, breath shallow, eyes flickering.

By his side was the little one, Ruby, nuzzling his soft belly. She greeted us with happy tweets and jumped into Hazel's arms. I smiled at the sight of the two before crouching beside the tyvarin, gently touching the side of his neck.

His eyes focused on me.

No fury. No orders. Just confusion.

Then pain.

Then... recognition.

He didn't speak – couldn't, not like this – but I saw it in the way his claws flexed, in the low rumble of his breath. The command chain was broken. He was free.

Hazel crouched beside me, her voice soft. "Will he be okay?"

"He will be lost. Like I was. But he will have a chance now. If his injuries heal." I got up and scanned the area. "I will hunt for him. We will leave him with supplies and a fire to restore his own. Then it is his choice whether to enter the lab and use the machine like I did or to stay a tyvarin. A free tyvarin. But first, help me take the collar off him."

I missed my old strength as we struggled to heave the collar from around his neck. Hazel helped as much as she could, while Ruby cheered us on, tiny purple wings flapping with excitement. By the time the collar finally dropped to the floor, we were breathing hard.

A low buzzing noise alerted me to an incoming drone.

"Hide," I hissed at Hazel, before swirling around to face the enemy. My wings unfurled, beating once, twice, remembering their function. I jumped into the air, half-expecting to crash, but my wings carried me like they always had.

I raced towards the drone while gathering fire inside my chest. It was still burning there, the fire the makers had cursed me with. Would I be able to use it in this form?

Only one way to find out.

When the drone came into reach, I reached deep and breathed...fire. A stream of turquoise flames shot at the drone, engulfing it. The buzzing stopped and the drone fell from the sky, shattering on the rocky slope below.

I pumped my fist in victory.

My mouth tasted of ash and acid, my lips were too hot, almost burned, but I had vanquished the enemy.

But more drones would follow. By now, the game makers had to know that we'd broken into the lab. It was time to leave.

I landed in front of Hazel with an uneven stumble. I needed to work on my flying skills.

"We have to go," I announced. "I will carry you down into the valley. Then I will hunt and bring some meat to the tyvarin, while you and the little one rest and recover."

"Are we going back to your cave?"

"It is too far just now. I want to stay close to the tyvarin, in case he needs more help. I thought I could leave him to his own devices, but... he is like me. I want to help him."

She put a hand on my arm. "I understand. And I agree with your decision. Although I don't like being parted from you."

"Neither do I. But it won't be for long. Now, let's find a place to shelter before more drones come."

I turned towards the ridge.

The sun was beginning to set behind the mountain peaks, casting long golden shadows across the stone. The air felt cleaner somehow. Like something had shifted beneath the skin of this world.

Freedom had begun.

And I had someone to share it with.

Tyvaron dropped off a huge leaf filled with berries and nuts along with a skinned leg of some kind of beast, before immediately departing again. We'd found a cave halfway down the mountains that he'd declared far enough from the lab to be safe. It was nowhere near as big as the cave he called home, but it would do for now.

It was strange to be alone. Not completely alone, Ruby was by my side. But he wasn't here. I'd spent the last two days - or had it been longer? - in Tyvaron's presence, rarely ever parted. And now that he had changed from a huge, intimidating dragon into someone a little more human-shaped, I was desperate to talk to him. To understand who he was now. To understand how I was supposed to feel about him.

Everything had changed.

I'd started to really like the dragon – admire him, even. I'd respected his strength, his protectiveness, his resilience. I had felt for all he'd endured, for the tragedy of what had been done to him. He was noble, in a strange, quiet way. And I had hoped for a better future for him, one where he was free.

But I hadn't pictured myself in that future. Not truly.

Now, he was still Tyvaron – but he was... possible.

He was still taller and broader than me by a good margin, but now he had a shape that was closer to mine. Arms and legs that ended in clawed fingers and scaled feet, yes – but they were hands I could hold, shoulders I could lean on. His body was still covered in that breath-taking mix of aquamarine and deep turquoise scales, but the plates across his chest and shoulders had formed into something like natural armour. Power, sculpted and gleaming, but wrapped in a shape I could touch without fear of being crushed.

His face...oh my. It was a blend of alien strength and startling beauty. Strong jaw, high cheekbones beneath a layer of fine, glimmering scales. No hair – just a crown of scales that shimmered subtly when the light hit it – and the two long, curved horns sweeping back from his head like obsidian blades. His eyes were golden. Bright. Deep. Reptilian, yes – but full of warmth.

His wings folded neatly down his back, their edges rough where wounds hadn't fully healed. A thick, lizard-like tail curled behind him for balance. He wore nothing – not a stitch, not a scrap. The machine had left him bare, every inch of him exposed in shimmering scale and alien strength.

And gods, he *should* have looked ridiculous. Or at least awkward. But somehow he didn't. He stood like he belonged in that body – regal and unashamed, as if clothes were the stranger concept.

He was beautiful. In a way that shouldn't have made sense. In a way that twisted my insides when I thought about him too long.

I pressed my hand to my chest, grounding myself in the feel of my own skin. At first, I'd been afraid of the dragon that had kidnapped me. But not anymore. Tyvaron didn't frighten me.

He stirred something else in me now, not fear. Something I wasn't sure I had words for. A quiet heat. A curiosity. The way I'd watched his lips move when he spoke. The way I'd imagined what it would be like to run my fingers across the scales that dusted his collarbones. To press my mouth to the hollow of his throat.

I wasn't just attracted to him. I was fascinated. Spellbound, even. Not by the beast he had been... but by the person he had always been beneath the metal, the scales, the pain.

And now that he had a form that made it possible – no, easy – to imagine standing beside him as an equal, to touch him, to *be* with him...

Fuck, what did that mean?

I wasn't sure if I was falling for him.

But I knew that if I was, I wouldn't fight it.

Not anymore.

But I was a fantasist. A dreamer. I dreamed most of

my life away, hoping for something better than what I had, and getting depressed when it never came to pass.

That was always the pattern. Highs that soared too fast. Lows that sank too deep. I'd get obsessed with something – a place, a person, an idea – and I'd chase it until it either broke me or slipped through my fingers. I'd idolise people who treated me badly, until everything escalated. Then I'd spiral. I'd think it was all my fault. That I wasn't enough. That I was too much.

Even before Kalumbu, I knew how dangerous hope could be.

I'd spent years learning to manage that. Therapy. Medication. Journalling. Meditation. I did the work. And I got better.

But there were still scars. Literally and otherwise.

Tyvaron hadn't asked about them. Not when he saw the pale lines on my thighs, or the larger ones across my arms. Maybe he hadn't noticed, or maybe he understood what they were and chose not to push. Or maybe he thought they were battle scars – which they were, in a way. A constant battle with my own brain. Either way, I was grateful. No pity. No questions I wasn't ready to answer. Just... acceptance.

But now?

Now he had a face I could kiss. Hands that could hold mine. Eyes that saw me like I mattered.

And it terrified me.

Not because of him.

Because of me.

What if I latched onto him the way I used to latch

onto the wrong people back home? What if this was just another fixation born out of trauma and adrenaline and survival?

What if he figured it out?

What if he didn't?

I pressed my face into Ruby's warm side, her scales cool but comforting. She didn't care about my baggage. She just liked my smell and the fact I wasn't Tyvaron's size.

"I don't want to mess this up," I whispered to her. "Whatever this is. I just want to be okay."

She chirped softly, curling tighter around me.

I let my eyes drift shut.

Tyvaron had said I was the reason he found himself again. That I helped free him.

What he didn't know – what I hadn't told him – was that he'd done the same for me.

Being here, with him, forced me to look at the parts of myself I usually ran from. The scars. The dreams. The guilt.

My priorities had shifted. I'd had to fight to survive, run from monsters, deal with life and death and evil overlords. I wasn't obsessing about my thoughts and memories all the time. I was *living* again. Focusing on the present, just like my therapist had always wanted me to. Back home, it had been easier to linger in the past, blame all my failures on it.

Suddenly, I was planning for the future.

And somehow, it didn't feel like too much anymore.

I wasn't healed. Not fully. But I was healing.

And maybe... just maybe...
This time, I wouldn't run.

I woke with a smile on my lips. I was warm and cosy and I had dreamt of flying, soaring through the sky, free as a bird. It had been the best dream I'd had in months.

I stretched like a cat, a squeal escaping from my throat.

Tyvaron laughed. My eyes shot open and I sat up quickly, suddenly very self-aware. He sat cross-legged on the other side of a fire he must have lit while I'd been asleep, watching me with a small smile. He'd wrapped a wide leather strap around his waist, reminding me of a kilt. I was glad he was no longer fully naked. It had been difficult not to stare.

"How..." A yawn interrupted my words. "How did it go?"

"The tyvarin was a little more conscious when I returned. I made him eat the meat I'd brought and built a fire. For some reason, we heal faster when we're close to flames. I promised I'd return tomorrow with more food."

"Where did you find your skirt?" I teased.

"I found another storage cave. It's just around the corner from here, actually. If I'd known, we could have set up camp there." He held up two metallic bags. "I found old rations. They should still be edible. If you want a change from meat and berries."

"Don't forget nuts. They make up a large part of my current diet."

He chuckled. "I am not sure what my diet should be. As Tyvaron, I only ate meat. Fresh, bloody, uncooked. Now, that thought does not feel appealing. I think I could eat raw meat if I had to, but imagining it roasted, cooked to perfection, slightly charred at the edges, makes my mouth water."

"Good thing we have both a fire and meat. Let me cook it for us this time. Do you have a stick I can use to hold it above the flames?"

Tyvaron grinned. "Too late. I have already prepared our meal. But I will let you do it next time, now that I know you'd like to cook for me."

From behind him, he produced two large leaves laden with thick slices of roasted meat. I didn't know what animal it had come from and I didn't want to know. He'd decorated it with a few berries. The thought of him garnishing our meal made me grin widely.

The meat was surprisingly tender, the berries a tart counterpoint. I took a bite and let out an involuntary moan.

Tyvaron stilled.

I opened one eye and caught the look on his face — the way his eyes had darkened slightly, heat flickering there that had nothing to do with the fire. I swallowed quickly.

"Too much?" I asked, lips twitching.

His voice was rough. "Not at all."

We ate in silence for a few moments, the crackle of the fire and the occasional chirp from Ruby – who was curled up in a mossy nest nearby, snoring with little puffs of smoke – the only sounds.

He took small bites, chewing slower than I expected. Almost like he was savouring every flavour. Watching him now, in his humanoid form, was different in every possible way. He was still too beautiful for my peace of mind – all sculpted lines and shimmering skin, horns catching the firelight like polished stone – but he looked more relaxed. Or maybe just less like he was one second away from collapsing.

"How do you feel?" I asked once we were both nearly done.

"Better," he said. "The shift exhausted me, but my strength is returning faster than expected. This form… it stabilises something inside me. The pain is dulled. The fire is easier to control."

"That's good."

He looked up. "And you?"

I blinked. "Me?"

"Yes. You've barely stopped since we left the cave. You've flown, climbed, faced a lab full of nightmares, freed a dragon, and… slept beside a monster." He said it softly, but there was a hint of steel beneath the words. "You've done all of that without breaking."

I fiddled with a berry on my plate. "I didn't say I wasn't breaking."

His gaze didn't waver. "But you kept going."

I shrugged. "That's kind of my thing. Keep going. Even when it sucks."

He tilted his head. "And before? When you weren't running from drones or fighting tyvarin. What did you do then?"

"I survived," I said eventually. "I worked as an archaeologist. Dig sites, cataloguing pottery shards, brushing sand off artifacts that hadn't been touched in thousands of years... Not as glamorous as people think. I spent most of my time alone, and honestly, I liked it that way."

Tyvaron said nothing, just listened.

"I didn't have many close friends. I was the weird one – the one who turned down parties to stay home with a documentary or a crochet hook. I liked crafting. I liked stories. Netflix binges and solitude. It wasn't a bad life. But it was small. Safe. Predictable."

I rolled a pebble between my fingers.

"And still, somehow, I wasn't happy. I kept hoping something would change. That something *would* find me – adventure, purpose, connection. Anything to shake me loose from... me."

A pause. I felt the truth clawing at the edge of my throat.

"And when it didn't, I started to spiral. I didn't sleep. I didn't eat much. I started thinking maybe I was the problem. That maybe I was just broken in a way that couldn't be fixed."

I looked up, meeting his eyes.

"Coming here – being thrown into this mess – it

was the worst thing that ever happened to me. And maybe also the best. Because now... I'm not pretending anymore. I'm *doing*. I'm fighting. I'm changing."

Tyvaron's voice was low and steady. "You were never broken. You were waiting."

"Waiting for what?"

"For someone who saw you," he said simply. "Really saw you."

My breath caught. He wasn't just being kind. He meant it.

We sat with that for a while, the silence settling again – this time, companionable. Comfortable.

Then I asked, "What do we do next?"

His eyes found mine. "That depends on you."

"Me?"

"You freed me. You helped me reclaim my form. You grounded me when I was losing myself. Whatever comes next – we face it together. But it begins with your choice. Do we return to my cave and hide from the masters? Do we seek out the other tyvarin, try and return them to their former selves? Start a rebellion? Or try and find a new home, leave everything behind, just the three of us?"

I stared into the fire. "I wish I had an answer. But I really don't know. Part of me wants to leave, escape, ignore everything. But we saw how confused, how broken the other tyvarin was. He needs help. If we left without helping him, what would that make us?"

"I am used to being a monster," he said softly. "But you are not."

"I don't want to be a monster either," I said. "And I don't want to be a coward."

"You've never been either."

"I came here naked and terrified, remember?"

"You came here naked and furious," he corrected gently. "You fought with a stick and protected a creature smaller than you. That is not cowardice. That is strength."

My throat tightened.

"I think... I want to try," I whispered. "To help the others. If there's even a chance they can be freed like you were – not just from their collars, but from the damage, the pain – then I want to be part of that. I *have* to be."

Tyvaron gave a slow nod, his golden eyes glowing like twin embers. "Then we will begin with him. The black-scaled tyvarin. We will stay nearby, offer what we can. If he chooses to trust us, we will help him reclaim what was lost. And from there... we will find the others."

"And if we can't?"

"Then we try anyway. Until we can no longer stand."

That pulled a laugh from me, tired and trembling and real.

"Alright, dragon boy. Let's save your people."

I looked at him across the fire, at the way the flames played across his scaled skin, casting shadows along the curve of his cheekbones and the strong lines of his jaw. He looked alien and familiar all at once – dangerous, powerful, yes – but also... mine.

He leaned forward, slow and deliberate, and placed his hand over mine.

"You already saved one."

And just like that, the fire between us was no longer just in the hearth.

I couldn't take my eyes off her. The firelight painted her skin gold. Her short hair was tangled from sleep, cheeks flushed with warmth and dreams. Tonight, all her defences were gone, no sarcasm to hide behind. Only truth. Only her.

I reached across the space between us. My fingers brushed hers. She didn't pull away.

"I don't know what tomorrow brings," she whispered. "But tonight... I don't want to think."

"You don't have to," I said, my voice low. "Let me think for you."

I pulled her closer.

Her breath caught as my hand slid up her arm, slow, reverent. She felt fragile compared to my hard, tough scales – but I had learned fragility was not weakness. She was made of scars and softness. Both mattered.

She leaned in. Our foreheads touched. My wing arched behind her, sheltering us.

"I've never done this," I murmured. "Like this. Not since I lost my body. My name."

Her eyes searched mine. "Do you want to wait?"

"No." I paused. "I want you. Crave you. I have ever since I first inhaled your scent in the forest. The beast in me didn't know why it wanted you, but it knew it had to have you."

I kissed her.

Her lips were soft, so very soft. She was all warmth and gentleness and home.

She melted into me. Her fingers curved against my bare back, exploring the contours of muscle and scale. I gasped against her lips, the sensation overwhelming – not just touch, but meaning. It had been lifetimes since anyone had touched me like this. Not in fear. Not in battle.

In trust.

My hands trembled as I guided her back, but I paused before laying her down. This was a cave – rough stone and shadows. She deserved better than rock against her spine.

"Wait," I murmured, brushing her hair from her face.

She looked up at me, breathless and flushed, but didn't protest when I gently tugged the makeshift skirt from her hips. I laid it down beside the fire, then turned to the walls, ripping a thick patch of moss free – soft, dry, and faintly warm from the fire's heat. I spread it carefully beneath the blanket, creating a crude but passable bedding.

Her gaze didn't leave mine once. She smiled – not at the makeshift bedding, but at the fact that I'd thought to make it for her. That I cared enough to try.

"You're full of surprises," she whispered.

"You haven't seen anything yet."

She sat down on the blanket and pulled her shirt over her head – slowly, sensually – baring herself to me without hesitation. Her skin was dusted with firelight, her curves impossibly perfect. Her nipples pebbled in the cooler air, and I couldn't help but drink in the sight of her.

I swallowed hard.

"You're beautiful," I said huskily.

Her eyes softened. "So are you."

I reached for the wide leather strap wrapped around my waist and loosened it. It slipped free with a soft sigh of fabric against scale, leaving me bare before her. I didn't hide myself – not from her. She'd seen the worst of me already. Now she could have everything.

I knelt between her legs and let her hands roam over me, guiding my own to her body. I cupped her breasts, brushing my thumbs across her nipples until she arched beneath me, her lips parting in a gasp. Then I lowered my mouth, licking and sucking gently until she trembled, fingers tangling in my hair.

She arched into me, hands clutching at my shoulders, urging me closer. The sound she made when I took her nipple into my mouth – that sound would be etched into my bones forever.

She was so alive beneath me. So present. So real.

And she wanted *me*. Not the dragon. Not the beast. Not the weapon. *Me*.

"You feel..." she murmured, voice caught between wonder and heat. "Fuck, you feel incredible."

I didn't answer with words. I kissed down her belly, trailing fire with my lips. When I reached her thighs, I paused – inhaling her, savouring her – then buried my mouth between her legs.

Her gasp shattered the stillness. Her body jolted as my tongue found her, teasing her clit with slow, deliberate circles. She was sweet and earthy, like the forest after rain, like something I had no words for – only need. I licked deeper, drawing moans from her throat that stirred something primal in me. Something reverent.

I was worshipping her.

Her thighs trembled beneath my hands, slick and open to me, her body humming with trust. Her hands gripped my shoulders, her back arching as I licked deeper. I felt her tense, then break apart around me, crying out my name – not my true one, not yet – but the name she'd known me by since the beginning. *Tyvaron.*

It still fit. But it wasn't the whole of me. Not anymore.

I kissed her thighs as she came down, holding her close, breathing with her. My own body ached, blood burning through me like wildfire, every instinct clawing for release – but I waited.

I wanted her to see. To know.

When her eyes fluttered open and she pulled me up for a kiss, there was no hesitation in her. Only hunger. Only heat. She looked at me – really *looked* – her hand sliding around my cock, slow and reverent. I hissed through my teeth. The touch was too much, too perfect.

Then she paused. Her brows lifted slightly, lips parting in what I could only describe as fascinated concern.

"Stars," she murmured, glancing from her hand to my face. "Are all dragon men built like *that*?"

A flush warmed her cheeks, but she didn't pull away. If anything, her grip tightened. She gave me a slow stroke that made my hips jerk despite myself.

I tried to speak – to reassure her, tease her, *something* – but I was too far gone, too stunned by the feel of her skin on mine, the sheer intimacy of it.

Hazel tilted her head, eyes narrowing thoughtfully. "It's... beautiful. And kind of terrifying." Her voice dropped to a whisper. "Do you think it'll fit?"

I let out a low growl, half-laugh, half-moan, pressing my forehead to hers.

"It *will*," I promised hoarsely. "If we go slow. If you want me."

"I *do*," she whispered. "Gods help me, I really do."

Then she drew me down into a kiss – and there was no more space between us, no more questions. Just heat, and trust, and the slow, sacred way we came together.

I braced myself above her, careful not to put too much weight on her body. My wings folded close, tail curled to one side.

"Tell me if I hurt you," I said, voice rough. "Or if I go too fast."

"You won't," she whispered. "I trust you."

That word again. Trust. It shattered something inside me. In a good way.

I lined myself up, dragging the head of my cock slowly through her slick folds, just to feel her, to memorise every inch of this moment.

Hazel gasped, hips twitching. "You're teasing me."

"Yes," I growled. "Because once I'm inside you... there's no going back."

"Good," she whispered. "I don't want to."

I eased forward, slowly, carefully. Her body resisted at first – then welcomed me with a heat so intense it nearly broke me. She was tight. So tight. I had to grit my teeth to keep from losing control.

Hazel clutched at my arms, fingernails digging into my scaled skin. Her breath hitched.

"Still okay?" I rasped.

She nodded quickly, then pulled me down into another kiss. "More."

I pushed deeper, inch by inch, watching her face the whole time. Her eyes fluttered shut, lips parted, cheeks flushed. Her thighs clenched around my hips, drawing me in. I bottomed out with a groan I couldn't hold back.

"Hazel," I said, my voice breaking on her name. "You feel like..."

"Like home?" she whispered.

"Yes."

I moved inside her – slow at first, savouring the stretch, the pull, the way our bodies aligned like they were always meant to. She moaned, hips lifting to meet mine, her breath catching with every stroke.

The world narrowed again. Not to pain or battle or blood.

To her.

To *this*.

Her hands roamed over my back, over the ridges of my shoulders and down my spine. She traced the scars there, the places where metal had once been forced into me. And not once did she flinch.

"You're perfect," she murmured. "Every part of you."

I buried my face in her neck, breath ragged. "I am trying very hard to believe you."

We moved together, the rhythm building slowly, each thrust deeper, more desperate. The cave echoed with the sounds of us – breath, movement, need. I could feel her getting close, her walls fluttering around me, her moans growing sharper.

"I've got you," I said, one hand sliding between us to stroke her clit in time with my thrusts. "Come for me, Hazel. I want to feel you let go."

And she did – with a cry that turned into a gasp, her body tightening around me, pulling me with her. The heat, the pressure, the emotion – it tore through me like lightning.

Pleasure surged through every nerve, more powerful than anything I'd ever felt, and then –

Something shifted in me, deep inside my mind. And something else was revealed, rising through the fog.

My name.

Not the one they gave me. The one I'd *lost*.

Fallin.

Fallin of Clan Varrna.

My orgasm tore through me as the name echoed in my mind, in my soul. I groaned her name, buried inside her, shaking with the force of it. Hazel held me, arms locked around my back, anchoring me to this moment, this truth.

I was free.

And I was *Fallin*.

Hazel's breath slowed beneath me, each inhale syncing with my own. Her fingers traced lazy circles on my back, grounding me in the aftermath. The cave, so cold and lifeless before, now felt like the heart of the universe – because she was here. Because *we* were here.

I rolled to the side carefully, bringing her with me so we remained tangled together. Her leg draped across mine. Her cheek rested against my chest.

"You're trembling," she whispered.

"I know." My voice came out raw, reverent. "Not from pain. Not anymore."

She pressed a kiss over my heart. "Then what is it?"

"I remembered."

Her head lifted slightly. "What?"

"My name." I cupped her cheek, tilting her face so I could see her eyes. "The one I had before the collars, before the masters and the blood and the fire. The name I was born with. The one they tried to erase."

Hazel stilled. "Tell me."

I swallowed. "Fallin. Fallin of Clan Varrna. That's who I was. That's who I *am*."

She repeated it softly, reverently. "Fallin."

Hearing it on her lips... it undid something in me. I hadn't realised how much I'd needed it. How much I'd longed for someone to speak that name and know it meant *me*.

Hazel smiled gently. "Fallin. I like it."

I leaned down, brushing my forehead to hers. "It means 'sky-blood' in the old tongue. I was named after my grandsire, and he after his grandsire. My people believed those with that name were destined to return from any fall. To survive. To rise again."

"Then it fits you perfectly," she said, curling closer. "Because you're still rising."

We lay there in the cave, the weight of the world held at bay. For a few breaths, there was no war. No past. Just her fingers tracing symbols across my chest. Just the warmth of her skin.

"I like this version of you," she said eventually. "But I think I'd still want you, no matter what shape you wore."

That nearly undid me all over again.

"I think," I whispered, "that I was always meant to find you. No matter how long it took."

And in the silence that followed, our fingers remained twined – two survivors remaking the world, one breath at a time.

I woke to warmth.

Not the flickering heat of firelight or the faint breath of morning sun filtering into the cave – but the deep, steady warmth of a body curled beside mine.

Fallin.

His arm was heavy around my waist, his breath soft and even against the back of my neck. One of his wings lay half-draped over us like a blanket, the edges twitching slightly with each exhale. His tail curled behind my knees. His presence was enormous, and yet I felt... safe. Cradled. Like the world outside didn't matter so long as he kept breathing beside me.

My body ached in the best possible ways.

I didn't move right away. Just stared at the cave wall and let it settle over me – what we'd done. What it meant. What it might mean.

No regrets. None. But my thoughts spun anyway.

Were we together now?

Was that what this was?

We'd fallen asleep tangled in each other, his arms around me like he'd been afraid I'd vanish if he let go. But we'd not talked about what had happened. No declarations had followed. No promises.

Was I his girlfriend now? No, I hated that word. *Partner* was much better.

Could he come to Earth? Would he even want to?

A huge, scaled alien dragon-man walking through Glasgow in a leather kilt probably wasn't going to go unnoticed. Assuming we ever got off this bloody planet. Assuming I even wanted to go back. Assuming... assuming so many things.

I sighed, soft and long. His arms tightened slightly, and I realised he was awake.

"I can hear you thinking," he murmured, voice still gravelly with sleep.

I smiled. "That loud, huh?"

"Like thunder." He shifted behind me, pressing his face into my shoulder for a moment before slowly propping himself up on one elbow. "Want to tell me what's making your mind race before it explodes?"

I rolled onto my back, staring up at the uneven ceiling. "Just... everything."

His gaze was steady. "Us?"

"Partly." I met his eyes. "I don't regret it. Any of it. But I don't know what comes next. I don't even know what's *possible*, Fallin. We're on a wild alien planet, your people are scattered, the game makers are still out there, wanting to kill us – and I've got no shoes."

That made him huff a quiet laugh. "The last part is most urgent, clearly."

I smiled, but didn't look away. "Are we... together now?"

He didn't answer immediately.

Instead, he reached for my hand, bringing it to his chest where his heart thudded strong beneath scale and skin.

"I don't know your species' word for what I feel," he said. "But I know I want to stay close. Wake beside you. Walk beside you. Fight and fly and burn beside you. If that means we're together, then yes. We are."

My heart did something strange and fluttery.

"I like that answer," I said.

"Good." His voice dropped, almost shy. "What do you want to do today?"

"Survive," I said dryly. "Make a plan. Figure out if we stay on Kalumbu or try to find a way off. If we help more tyvarin or try to find allies."

"We start small," he said. "We hunt. We feed the black one again. We check his wounds. Then we find higher ground. I want to see the sky."

"Your sky?"

He smiled faintly. "One day, maybe. But for now – this one."

His wing unfurled and curled gently around me again.

"Come," he said. "The world is waiting."

This time, we went hunting together. If you can call collecting berries and nuts hunting. I picked as many as I could while Fallin was searching for game nearby. I heard the fight from afar, but before I could get worried, he flew into my field of vision, holding a small, bloody carcass. I didn't look too closely at what kind of beast he'd killed.

"Will that be enough for us and the other tyvarin?" I asked when he landed in front of me.

"I'm hoping that the tyvarin will be well enough to fly to my cave today. He is in constant danger if he stays that close to the lab. Once we're back at the cave, I'll go hunting again. I know that area much better than this. It won't take long to find a beast big enough to sate the tyvarin's appetite and our own."

Instead of returning to our temporary cave, we had breakfast in the forest, munching berries and nuts. Ruby surprised us both when she dropped some nuts on a flat rock in front of her and blew fire on them. They cracked in the heat, releasing the scent of roasted cinnamon. She nudged my hand as if to offer me to try her creation, pride glimmering in her eyes.

I bit into the softened nut and could barely hold back a sigh of pleasure.

"That is utterly delicious," I said. It almost sounded like a moan. "Thank you, Ruby."

She chirped, looking very pleased with herself. Tyva- no, Fallin laughed and snatched one of the toasted nuts before the little dragon could devour them all. Ruby chittered happily and exhaled a burst of fire on the last remaining berries.

"Ruby, no!" I shouted, but it was too late. Only a

smouldering mess of charred berries and sticky juice remained.

"I guess that's breakfast over," Fallin said with a chuckle. "Are you ready to head back up the mountains? I should be strong enough to fly us all the way today."

I wiped my sticky hands on a leaf and stood, brushing crumbs from my makeshift skirt. "Let's do it."

Fallin wrapped his arms around me from behind, his chest firmly pressed against my back. His tail snaked across my waist for safety. For a moment, I imagined what else this tail could do. I was glad he couldn't see my face. His wings flexed, testing the wind, and then we were airborne. Ruby followed us with joyful chitters, clearly excited to be joining us on this adventure.

The flight felt different this time. Easier. More controlled. He was stronger now, steadier. I could feel it in the way he moved – confident, graceful. Like the skies were truly his again. The wind brushed through my hair and I was almost glad it was not as long as it used to be. More practical. Yes, that was the way to think about it. Be positive.

The sun hadn't risen far, but the mountains shimmered gold and red beneath us. The view stole my breath, even as my thoughts turned heavier with each beat of his wings.

I wasn't sure what we'd find. For some reason, I suddenly had a bad feeling about it all.

The slope came into view. The place we'd left him – the other tyvarin. My stomach twisted.

Fallin landed softly, releasing me from his secure grip. Ruby darted ahead, chirping once, then falling silent.

He lay exactly where we'd left him, but something was changed. The fire was out. The moss around the tyvarin was cold. And his chest no longer rose.

Fallin reached him first. He knelt beside the other dragon, laying a hand on the scaled neck. No pulse. No glow. No warmth.

"Too late," he said quietly.

I didn't know what to say. We'd tried. He'd tried.

"We freed him," I whispered. "And then he died. Why? That shouldn't have happened."

Fallin's wings drooped, the weight of the moment settling on his shoulders. He examined the dragon, running his hands over the obsidian scales. Yesterday, they had been shiny, filled with life. Now the spark of life had been extinguished.

Fallin suddenly snarled. "Look here. It wasn't the injuries that killed him." His eyes were ice cold as he looked at me. "He was murdered."

I looked at where he pointed. A thin line sliced through the tyvarin's throat, barely visible, stained with dried blood. His throat had been cut.

I sucked in a sharp breath. My eyes burned. We were too late. While we'd been sleeping safely in our cave, then having a leisurely breakfast in the forest, this dragon had been attacked.

"He died alone," Fallin whispered. "I wasn't here for him. I didn't defend him. I didn't share his last moments. I didn't listen to his final breath."

I crouched beside him, brushing a hand gently over the tyvarin's shoulder. "You had no choice. If we'd stayed here, we may be dead as well. The game makers clearly know what you've done. They will be coming after you."

He rose to his feet, his jaw set, determination shining in his eyes. A solitary tear ran down his scaled face. "Let them come."

I took his hand and together, we looked upon the dead tyvarin. I felt like I should say something, mark his passing in some way, but I knew nothing about the dragon. He had been strong and formidable when he'd fought Fallin, but we didn't even know his name.

"May you rest in peace," I whispered beneath my breath. "And may you be the last tyvarin to ever die alone."

Fallin squeezed my hand. "The masters will pay for this. I swear it."

A ray of sunshine burst from the clouds, bathing the obsidian dragon in warm light. It was as if the universe marked our words.

I breathed in deep. "We will make sure no one else ends up like this. I will be by your side every step of the way."

He glanced up towards the distant cliffs, where the

sky turned pale blue behind the broken horizon. "We'll go back to the lab. Use the network again – but this time, we use the collars to call them. Show them how I was changed by the machine. Offer sanctuary. A choice. To use the machine themselves, if they want it. Or freedom in their current form. And then, war against the masters."

Fallin exhaled, slow and steady. "Before I call them, I need to know if I can change back into Tyvaron. To battle the masters, I need to be at my full strength."

"Are you sure about this?"

He nodded grimly. "There is no other way. I had hoped to wait with this, but I cannot. If I offer the others the choice of using the machine, they must know all potential consequences."

Before I could say another word, he took a step back. His hand brushed mine briefly – a silent goodbye, or maybe a promise. Then he moved away from me, into the open space where the wind tugged at his leather belt and the sun glinted off the scales that shimmered across his skin.

I held my breath.

He closed his eyes. His whole body stilled.

And then it began.

The change rippled through him – scale and flesh, bone and light – his outline blurring into something vast and winged. His back arched, arms extending, wings unfurling like sails catching a rising wind. The air around him shimmered, charged with something ancient and powerful.

No pain. No struggle.

This time, it was his choice. And he was victorious.

I took a step closer, shielding my eyes as his dragon form solidified – familiar now, but still magnificent. The turquoise and aquamarine scales caught the sunlight like gemstones, every motion fluid, natural. His horns swept back elegantly from his brow, his eyes glowing with quiet resolve.

He was still him. Still Fallin.

But now... all of him.

And I couldn't stop staring.

"You did it," I whispered. "Did it hurt?"

"No." His voice boomed with the strength of Tyvaron, but held the warmth I'd come to know of Fallin. "Hop on. I will fly us to the lab."

"To call your kin?"

He shook his head, smoke rising from his nostrils. "To call *our* kin. The lost. The broken. The waiting. If we move fast, we can reach them before they're hunted again."

It was time to begin something new.

FALLIN

The lab lay abandoned, the sentries gone. Its corridors smelled of cold metal and old blood, though less than before. Perhaps it was my senses, dulled by purpose. Or perhaps something had shifted in me. I was no longer a weapon walking through his birthplace. I was a survivor returning to reclaim it.

I'd shifted back to my smaller shape just outside, once I'd made sure there were no guards to deal with. It was reassuring to know how easy it was to move between forms, but at the same time, I was very aware of how my larger shape was not the one I had been born in. It had been forced upon me. Maybe one day, when we were far from here, I could bury Tyvaron once and for all.

Hazel walked beside me, her expression tight, alert. Ruby darted ahead, snout occasionally brushing the walls as if seeking out old ghosts. They didn't scare her. Nor me. Not anymore.

We reached the control room with no resistance. No drones. No defence systems. Just the low, ever-present hum of buried power. I approached the central console and placed my hand flat against the interface. The machine came to life instantly.

"Yesterday, I removed the masters' control over the collars, but I think there is still a residual link to the tyvarin that I can exploit. If not, I will have to take control of the collars once more, but I would rather avoid it. I don't know what that would do to them when they've only just realised that they're free."

I started changing settings and adjusting frequencies, the system's AI guiding me in my task.

Hazel moved closer, watching over my shoulder. "What are you doing?"

"There's a beacon in every collar – a failsafe, meant to recall us in emergencies. I can rewrite its signal. Tell them to come, not as weapons... but as allies."

I called up the collar network. The map reappeared – thirty-one signals still active, scattered like blood drops across the jagged terrain of Kalumbu. I adjusted the coordinates, anchoring them to a plateau a few ridgelines west of the lab. A place I remembered from my early patrols – big enough for this many tyvarin to gather, high enough to not harbour any monsters that could be a threat, and far from any area where Trials contestants usually roamed. We'd be in full view of drones and satellites, but that could not be helped. The game makers already knew that I had regained control of my own mind and that I had freed my fellow tyvarin. But they did not know what I intended to do next.

I wrote the message.

This is Tyvaron. I set you free. I have changed to who I used to be. You can as well. Come if you choose. You will be met in peace. I will explain everything.

A single pulse of energy surged from the console. Not a command. A call.

It was done.

The plateau was wide and weathered, marked by age and the elements but still standing strong. We reached it by midday. The sun hung pale and gold above, casting long shadows over the stone. A few low bushes were dotted around, bent and twisted by the wind. Hazel helped me gather fuel for signal fires while Ruby busied herself collecting sticks and dropping it proudly at our feet. The location ping I'd encoded in the message would lead them in this general area and the fires would show them where to land. They were also a sign that it was really me who had sent out the call. The masters wouldn't bother with something as simple as a fire. They would use machines and pain.

Knowing they would not recognise me in this form, I shifted into Tyvaron once more. The change came easy and faster than before. Each time I shifted, I became *more*. More than the sum of two halves. I was Tyvaron and I was

Fallin. And someone new. The person Hazel had fallen in love with. The one who was going to be her mate.

I started the first blaze with a breath of fire. The smoke rose in a thin column, curling skyward like a banner.

Hazel stared into the flames. "Do you think they'll come?"

"I know they will."

She looked doubtful but didn't argue. Instead, she built a second fire, smaller. A comfort fire.

The first arrival came before the smoke could fully clear. A shape appeared in the sky – dark and fast, wings slicing the air. I tensed instinctively... but it landed without aggression.

A young tyvarin. Slightly smaller than me, deep green with silver accents. His eyes glowed faintly, and his movements were slow. Hesitant. He didn't speak.

Hazel didn't back away. She stepped forward, palms visible. "You're safe," she said gently. "No one's going to hurt you."

He stared into her eyes as if searching for proof that she was not a threat. Satisfied, he curled up on the ground. His collar was still attached, but it was lifeless and cold.

More arrived over the next hour – in pairs, alone, injured or confused. Some circled overhead for a long time before daring to land. Most were silent, but I could see the transformation in their eyes. Their minds were clearing.

A few remembered names. One looked at me and said *Krexya,* then choked up before he could speak again. Another wept openly when Ruby perched on his arm and chirped at him. They remembered the little one.

Hazel moved between them with cautious grace. They stared at her in wonder and confusion, as if they didn't know what or who she was, but also sensed that she was important somehow. That she was the pebble who had first hit the lake's surface, creating waves that were still rolling onto the shore.

She didn't try to fix them. She didn't pretend to understand them. She simply stayed and comforted them. That was more than they had ever experienced since their capture and transformation.

I was looking out for some tyvarin in particular, the ones I had fought with regularly, but only two of them turned up. I didn't dare think of what had happened to the others.

As we waited for more to arrive, Hazel put her hand on my neck as we observed the crowd of tyvarin. Her other hand held Ruby, who was fast asleep on her shoulder, snout twitching in dreams.

"They came," she said softly.

"They did."

"Do you think they'll want to stay?"

"I think they want to hope," I replied. "That's enough."

Later, we would take those who wished it back to

the lab. Offer them the machine. The others could stay here – safe, watched over, fed.

And after that?

We would see.

But right now, the winds carried no command. The skies bore no drones. And in the firelight, for the first time in generations, the tyvarin were together.

Free.

When the sun began its slow descent and the fires had burnt to smouldering embers, there were twenty-six tyvarin squeezed onto the plateau. I roared once to gain their attention, then I told them my story. I showed them the collar we'd taken from the fallen obsidian tyvarin. I told them about my rebellion, how I'd refused an order, how I'd met Hazel, and how I'd entered the machine. The chance to shift. To remember. To choose. I told them there was no path forward without choice.

And then I shifted into Fallin to show them what was possible. They gasped, shook their wings, their eyes burning with desire to reclaim their past and their future.

Not one of them left.

One by one, they flew to the lab and entered the machine. I guided the first few through the process until they had recovered enough to help the next tyvarin.

Not all of them looked like me when they emerged

from the lab. Some had no wings, others had fur rather than scales, others were much smaller or bigger. But there were three that were of my species, one female and two males. I did not know them, did not remember them, but that did not matter. We were kin. I knew they would fight by my side because of that alone.

I watched the shifted tyvarin as they gathered in small groups, talking, slowly relearning social skills. Some had separated from the group, preferring to be alone, while a few more had shifted back into their tyvarin forms, finding perches along the rim of the plateau or curling up beside newly lit fires. The transformations had exhausted them – some had emerged dazed, others shaken, and a few quietly weeping when memories returned. Still, they had all chosen this. Chosen freedom.

And now they looked to me.

Hazel returned to my side, Ruby on her shoulder once more, still sleepy but clearly aware that something important was happening. The little one chirped, then tucked her nose beneath her wing.

I spoke without turning to Hazel. "We need a plan."

She nodded. "You've gathered them. Now what?"

"We cannot win in a direct assault. The masters are not on the planet's surface. They are somewhere in space, orbiting Kalumbu. They don't need to be here, they have their drones and satellites. But what we do have..." I glanced behind me at the sleeping tyvarin, glowing softly in the firelight, "...is unpredictability. We were meant to be mindless. Tools. They'll never expect strategy from us. They don't know what's happening. Let's take them by surprise."

Hazel crouched beside a flat stone and began sketching with a bit of charred wood. "So what do we do? Sabotage? Disruption?"

"Yes." I crouched next to her. "We turn them blind. Destroy as many drones as we can. Attack any vessel or guards they send. Until they have no choice but to come here in person."

"Do you think they will actually come?"

"I am not sure," I admitted. "But it is the best we can do from here. We cannot fly to the space station. tyvarin are strong, but we cannot survive without air. Maybe we can find a way to disrupt them through their own technology, here in the lab and elsewhere."

She reached out and gently touched the side of my neck. "Maybe some of the tyvarin have the skills we need? If they remember them from their previous lives."

Her touch grounded me. Steadied the fire inside me.

We sat in silence, thinking, trying to come up with strategies for a situation that seemed impossible. As I racked my brain on how we could defeat the monsters who had created us, I scanned the far ridges.

And then I saw it.

A flicker of silver on the horizon. Not a star. Not a tyvarin.

A drone.

Hovering.

Watching.

I bared my teeth. "We've been spotted."

Hazel rose quickly, her expression hardening. "What do we do?"

"We destroy it."

Smoke would rise again soon – not from signal fires this time, but from war.

I didn't sleep at all that night. The dragons had destroyed the drone before it could get too close, but it had been a reminder that the game makers were never far away. They were watching us. And they were probably working on plans to destroy us at this very moment.

I dozed fitfully and only Fallin's strong arms stopped me from giving up on sleep and pacing around the plateau. He got up at some point and didn't return, likely plagued by the same restlessness as me. When dawn rose over the mountain ridge, I was almost relieved to finally get up and spring to action.

The camp was slowly waking, with tyvarin and shifted-tyvarin stretching and yawning everywhere. Fallin was crouched at the edge of the plateau with one of the newly shifted dragons. They were deep in discussion, gesturing at a rough map scratched into the dirt with a claw. Ruby was perched on a boulder beside them, tail flicking like a tiny general waiting to be given her orders.

I stretched, wincing at the stiffness in my limbs. Sleeping curled up between dragon bodies did have a certain comforting warmth – like being wrapped in breathing stone – but it wasn't exactly ergonomic.

Did this planet have beds? And if not, could we build one?

As I walked over, Fallin looked up. He smiled, but he looked tired and exhausted.

"How many noticed the drone last night?" I asked quietly.

"Too many," he replied. "It caused a few to panic. One nearly took off again."

"Have there been any others?"

He nodded. "One, just before dawn. I destroyed it. But it will not be the last. We have to assume we're being tracked constantly."

I crouched beside the crude map. It was surprisingly detailed – Fallin's memory for terrain was unnervingly good. "So what's the plan?"

He pointed at three areas on the map. "We're splitting into wings. Small groups. Each will scout and destroy any surveillance tech they encounter. If we're lucky, we'll blind the game makers in key sectors. We'll also keep guards here for any drones sent to investigate the plateau. If we can take down enough, we'll force them to divert resources."

"Won't that just make them retaliate faster?"

"Maybe. But they'll be reacting to us, not controlling us." He looked at the tyvarin beside him, a lean male with golden scales and no wings. "Kareth here remembers how to use signal jammers. He was... a technician once. He's about to head to the lab to scavenge for any tech we can use."

Kareth didn't speak, but he gave me a solemn nod. I returned it, oddly touched.

"You're building an army," I said.

"I'm building a future." Fallin reached for my hand. "One where we are not hunted. None of us were born on this planet, but maybe we can finally make it our home. A safe home without others to control us. A place where we make the rules."

I squeezed his fingers, then pulled away gently. "What do you need me to do?"

He hesitated. "Keep the fire warm. Not all tyvarin are ready to join our mission. They will stay here to recover. Keep them steady. I need their minds calm. Your presence helps more than you realise."

"Sure you don't just want me to babysit dragons?"

Fallin wrinkled his scaled brow in confusion. "There are no baby dragons here. And some of them will be lying or standing."

I rolled my eyes and stood. "It's a human expression."

His eyes twinkled with mirth. "I know what babysitting means."

I repressed the urge to give him the finger and instead walked off with my head held high, looking for those who needed some company.

Throughout the day, I worked among the gathered tyvarin, most of them still adjusting to their new forms or memories. Some of those who'd recovered quickly had hunted and brought mountains of meat, along with scavenged items like blankets, emergency rations and first aid supplies from the lab. I handed out food, wrapped bandages where I could, and listened – really listened – when they spoke, even if the words came slowly, fragmented by trauma. Ruby trailed behind me, chirping greetings and occasionally stealing bits of roasted meat.

When a young female tyvarin started to cry – overwhelmed by the memories of her family, her old life, her lost name – I simply held her scaled hand and sat with her until the storm passed. No words. Just presence.

That's what Fallin had asked of me. And it was enough.

I felt needed. I had an important task and I relished in making the world a little better. My job back home had never quite given me that feeling. I'd loved finding artifacts, but a few newly discovered Bronze Age sherds didn't have an impact on people's lives. Only my own. Here, I did more than work towards my own goals and accomplishments. I was helping the tyvarin. I was making a difference.

As the sun reached its peak, I climbed to the edge of the plateau and looked out across the wide, broken land. Somewhere out there, a storm was brewing. But here, just for now, we had carved out a breath of stillness.

And we would defend it. With fire. With wings. With hope.

The peace didn't last.

I'd just knelt beside one of the tyvarin – an older one with scars across his back and a wing that hadn't quite healed – when Ruby let out a sharp chirp. A warning.

I stood immediately, scanning the horizon. A flicker of motion caught my eye, a sliver of sunlight that was too bright to be natural.

A drone.

It hovered low this time, below the clouds, its metallic body gleaming faintly. It kept a distance from us, not approaching, just...watching.

The others noticed it too. A ripple of unease spread across the plateau. A few tyvarin tensed, wings half-lifted. Others backed away, expressions blank with confusion or fear.

Before anyone could move, a crackling sound came from the drone, followed by a male voice.

"We have def-"

It didn't get to finish its message.

A tyvarin – one of the younger ones who preferred to stay in his dragon form – launched himself into the air with a furious roar. The drone began to rise, but it was too slow. A heartbeat later, he slammed into it with his full weight. The machine crumpled, sparks shooting into the air as they tumbled down in a tangled mess of metal and fury.

The dragon roared again, ripping the remains apart before spitting a final burst of fire onto what was left.

The others roared in approval, but I didn't join in.

I couldn't.

Because that voice... it hadn't sounded threatening. It had been a message, I was sure of it. Maybe a call for parley? Maybe the game makers had an offer for us?

I turned to Fallin, who had appeared at my side during the commotion, his eyes narrowed. His tail wrapped around my waist protectively while he scanned me from top to bottom, as if to reassure him that I was alright.

"Did you hear what it said?" I asked.

"I did."

"They weren't attacking. They were trying to talk."

He didn't answer right away. "It could be a trick."

"You don't trust them," I said.

He stepped back, hands gesticulating wildly. The sudden cold around my waist where his tail had been seeped all the way to my heart.

"Of course I don't!" he snapped. "They are the enemy! They did this to us! They have brought us nothing but pain and misery! You don't know them like I do. They are twisted, deceitful, and always searching for new ways to make our lives hell. Whatever they had to say, I'm glad the tyvarin didn't let them finish. Their words are poison. Nothing but poison."

Smoke rose from his nostrils and mouth, his wings stretched fully extended behind him, quivering with fury. I hated seeing him this angry, this upset – but I also understood his point.

I gently put my hand on his arm, and when he didn't react, I pulled him into my arms, gently running my hands over the hard base of his wings.

"Can we go away for just a short while?" I whispered softly. "I love taking care of the tyvarin, but it's all a bit too much. I'm not used to being surrounded by this many people all the time. I need a moment of privacy, just the two of us." I pressed my cheek against the scales on his chest, soaking in his warmth. He didn't say anything, but he wrapped his arms and wings around me, enveloping me in a cocoon of his scent and attention.

"I feel really selfish right now," I muttered after a while of simply enjoying his closeness. "They need us. I-"

"No," he growled. "I am sorry. I have not taken proper care of you. I have given you tasks without asking you about your wellbeing. How this is all affecting you. For a moment, I slipped back into being Tyvaron, ordering others around, only focused on the end goal – the masters' goal – without considering the individuals' interests and welfare."

He moved his hands to my bum, squeezed once

almost playfully, as if to lighten the mood, then lifted me up until I wrapped my legs around his waist, ready for flight.

"Let's fly. Hold on tight."

We took off without looking back. The tyvarin would be fine without us for a while.

The wind met us immediately, sharp and clean, tugging at Hazel's hair as we rose above the plateau. I angled my wings west, towards a place I remembered from my patrols – a rocky outcrop overlooking a sheer drop into a forest of orange-leaved trees. It was quiet there. High enough to give us warning of approaching drones, isolated enough to give us some privacy from the others.

Hazel leaned into me, her cheek against my collar-bone, her hands clutched into the scales of my back. I loved feeling her curled around me like this. My cock was hard against her abdomen. Did she know? Was she feeling the effect she had on me?

I landed softly atop the ridge and set her down with care, my hands reluctant to let go.

She turned slowly, taking in the view – jagged peaks in the distance, birds and other animals chasing each other in the forest's canopy below. "It's beautiful," she said finally.

"So are you," I replied without thinking.

She gave me a look – half amusement, half affection – and sat down on a patch of moss that had soaked in enough sun to be warm. I folded my wings and sat beside her, our legs brushing.

For a moment, there was peace again. No masters. No collars. Just air and sky and her.

"I miss silence," she said quietly. "Real silence. The kind that doesn't mean something awful is lurking just out of sight."

"I'm sorry I can't give you that yet."

"You give me more than enough." She leaned her head on my shoulder. "I just needed this. You. Us. Here. Without anyone asking anything of us."

My arm circled her waist. "You'll always have me."

She smiled at that.

Hazel didn't speak for a long time. She simply leaned into me, her cheek pressed to my shoulder, her breath calm and steady. The sun warmed our backs and the wind rolled past in slow, lazy gusts. I could sense forest creatures in the branches above us and in the ground below, but they knew better than to disturb a tyvarin and his mate.

For a few precious clicks, I let myself forget everything.

The war. The masters. The sky full of drones.

Right now, there was only this. Her.

She turned her face up towards me and whispered, "I used to spend whole weekends curled up with tea and a book. Or a ball of yarn."

I blinked. "Yarn?"

"Crocheting," she said with a small smile. "You use a hook to knot string into fabric. I started with coasters and a scarf, but then I went to craft groups and learned to make more difficult things. Soft things. Warm things. Things that don't bite." She reached out and traced one of the scales on my arm, just above the elbow. "You are... the opposite of soft. But you make me feel safe."

A strange sound escaped me – not quite a laugh, not quite a sigh. I rested my forehead against hers, inhaling the familiar scent of her skin, smoke and berries and something uniquely Hazel.

"I have no softness," I murmured. "But I can learn to be warm. For you."

Her hands found my jaw, cool against my flushed skin. "You already are."

We kissed then – slow, easy, unhurried. Not desperate like before, not laced with adrenaline or fear. Just lips on lips, the meeting of two beings who'd chosen this moment, this stillness. Her tongue brushed mine and the spark that always lived between us flared quietly, more ember than flame, but it would burn all the same.

When we parted, she stayed close, her nose brushing mine.

"I don't know what we're walking into," she whispered. "But I'm glad I'm not doing it alone."

"You never will be."

"What will happen to us?" she asked, her voice catching as if she didn't want to hear the answer. "What are we?"

"I have barely dared to think the word," I admitted. "But I think it is time you heard it. I don't know if your people, your *hoomahns*, use it in the same way but-"

"Say it."

I kissed her forehead once more. "You are my mate. My one and only mate, sent to me from across the stars. The one who freed me. The one who made me whole. The one who saved me, body and soul, wings and heart. Forever." I took a deep breath, watching her flushed cheeks, her wide eyes, her parted lips, trying to see if she understood what I meant.

"Hazel... I want to be with you, now and forever."

"Mate." She tasted the word, slow and deliberate. "Mates. I never thought I'd find someone I'd want to share my life with. I was always so independent, so keen not to get attached to anyone. To hurt from previous encounters. But now, with you..." She smiled and it lit up her face like sunshine bursting through dark clouds. "I can see us together, forty years from now, sitting on the top of a cliff, wrinkles and all, watching the sunrise. I only met you a few days ago, but I feel like I know you. Like I've always known you."

"I feel the same," I admitted. "We may be from

different species, but I know your heart, Hazel, my mate. And it beats in the same rhythm as my own."

We kissed again, slower this time, as if to seal the bond we'd just formed.

"I want to claim you," I said breathlessly when we broke apart. "In the way of my people."

Her lips were swollen, her eyes sparkling. I could never get tired of admiring her. My mate.

It felt unreal still. I had felt it from the start, I'd come to realise, even as Tyvaron, chained and feral. It was why I had captured her in the forest, taken her to my cave. As the beast Tyvaron, I hadn't known how to proceed. She'd been so tiny compared to my massive tyvarin size. It had been an impossibility. But from the moment I'd shifted to become me, Fallin, I'd known that she was mine. My mate, now and forever, stars-given, earth-set.

"And what way is that?" she asked. Did she know how alluring her fluttering eyelashes were?

"In the air. Naked, free, together. Will you allow me to claim you, mate?"

"Mate. I love it so much when you say it. Do it again."

"Mate," I repeated with a smile. "Mate. Mate. Is that enough for now?"

"For the moment."

"And will you let me claim you?"

She laughed. "Obviously. But please promise to not let me fall."

"Never."

Hazel stood, her body lit by golden sun and soft wind, and began to untie her makeshift blanket-dress. Her fingers trembled only a little. I watched, stunned, as she peeled it away and laid it across a dry patch of moss, then looked up at me with mischief burning in her gaze.

"Well?" she asked, a challenge in her tone. "You said 'naked, free, together.' Get to it."

I didn't need telling twice.

My fingers went to the leather belt around my waist – a poor excuse for clothing, really – and let it fall. She was already watching me with open curiosity, no shyness in her gaze now. I saw the flush on her cheeks, the way her breath caught when she looked at me fully.

She stepped towards me, fingertips brushing down my chest, over the faint shimmer of scales, the ridged muscle beneath. Her touch was reverent. "You're beautiful," she whispered.

I wasn't used to being described that way. Powerful, monstrous, deadly – yes. But beautiful?

I bent low to kiss her, slower this time, deeper. Then scooped her up in my arms with ease, one arm under her knees, the other supporting her back. "Are you ready?"

"Yes," she said simply.

I stepped to the edge of the outcrop. The world dropped away beneath us – forest, cliffs, the sky itself unfolding into a canvas of gold and flame.

And then I leapt.

She gasped once, then clutched tighter, but I felt no fear in her body. Only exhilaration. Trust.

The wind caught my wings. I beat them hard once, twice, and we soared.

Not high – not into the clouds – but in wide, sweeping arcs above the trees, over the river that glittered like molten glass, across the broken ridges where the land itself seemed to be scarred.

She was laughing. Real laughter, not the brittle kind that came from stress or exhaustion. It wrapped around me like starlight. And I laughed too.

"This is claiming?" she shouted over the wind.

"This is the start of it!" I called back.

I found a current and rose sharply, wings burning, heart thundering. I tipped us sideways and she squealed, legs tightening around my waist, her hands burying themselves in my hair.

And then – at the highest point of our arc – I slowed, hovered.

Kissed her again.

It was clumsy, wind-whipped, breathless – but it was ours.

She pulled back, lips shining, eyes alight with joy. "I never thought I'd fall for someone with scales."

I grinned, heart soaring. "I never thought I'd fall for anyone at all."

I'd never done a sky claiming before – it was reserved only for mates – but my ancestral memory guided me. I adjusted my wings to catch the updraft, keeping us stable in the air. Then I wrapped my tail around her waist as an anchor, to give her a sense of safety. I would never let her fall, but I knew she wasn't used to flying. Not yet.

I gently rotated her until she was facing me. She instinctively wrapped her legs around my waist while her arms snaked around my neck. I held her hips, steadying her.

My cock was hard and ready, pushing against her belly.

I tried to make my wings beat as smoothly as possible, keeping us in place without moving with the wind.

Her body shifted against mine, a slow grind that made stars burst behind my eyes. My cock slid against her, hot and aching. The sensation was maddening – friction, heat, closeness, but not yet enough.

Her breath caught. "You're... big."

I froze, only just.

She laughed softly, breathless. "I didn't say stop. I said big."

I met her gaze. "Are you sure?"

Hazel's lips brushed my jaw. "More than sure. I want all of you, Fallin. Everything."

I angled my hips carefully. Slowly. Gently. She shifted to welcome me, arms wrapped tight around my shoulders, eyes locked on mine.

And then I was inside her.

She gasped – and so did I. The world narrowed to the place where our bodies joined, where heat and trust and love fused into something holy.

Her nails dug into my back. I felt her legs tighten,

heels digging into my lower back as she pulled me closer, deeper.

The sky spun.

I moved in her slowly at first, testing what the wind would allow, how best to balance us without disrupting the rhythm. But Hazel... Hazel was glorious. She moved with me, met every thrust with her own, her breath coming in soft gasps against my neck. Her full breasts rubbed against my chest, her nipples as hard as my cock.

We didn't speak – there were no words for this. For flying and fucking and falling in love all at once.

Her mouth found mine again and again, clumsy and perfect kisses, devouring my restraint.

She was close. I could feel it – the way her thighs trembled around me, the way her hands clenched at my shoulders.

"I'm here," I rasped. "I've got you. Don't hold back."

She came with a cry muffled against my throat, her entire body trembling in my arms. And I held her through it, wings wide and steady, heart threatening to break with how much I loved her.

The release hit me like a lightning strike, hot and brutal and bright.

I groaned her name into her mouth as I came, pouring my release into her waiting folds. She whispered to me, words blown away by the wind, stroked my head, curled her fingers around my horns, until the last waves ebbed away and I could breathe again.

We hovered in the air, our bodies bare, pressed together above a world that had tried to kill us both.

She was my mate.

And I was hers.

And for that single, perfect moment – nothing else existed.

We sat side by side on a large rock until the shadows grew longer and Ruby chirped once from the edge of the outcrop, where she'd curled up like a cat. The warmth began to fade, and I shivered slightly.

"We should probably get back," I said with a sigh. "We've been away for too long."

Fallin caressed my cheek, the tiny scales on his fingers tickling my skin. "We needed this. The claiming made us stronger. We need to be as strong as possible for the upcoming war."

I shivered again, this time not from the cold.

We'd had a moment of escape, a few hours to breathe and recover. Now we had to return to reality.

I looked down at the stunning landscape below, the endless forest, the stone pillars rising in the distance. All of this could be our home, one day. If we managed to defeat the game makers.

And then I saw it.

A flicker on the horizon. Not a drone like before – this one was smaller, slower.

"Fallin-"

"I see it." He jumped to his feet.

"What is it?"

"It's an old model. They don't have the defensive capabilities the new drones have. This one can only watch."

"Maybe there's a reason they sent this one," I mused. "Maybe it's a message?"

We stood frozen, watching the drone draw closer – a slow, deliberate approach, not the erratic hover of a scout, not the aggressive spin of an attack unit. It moved like it had purpose. Like it wanted us to see it.

Fallin stepped in front of me, wings flaring slightly, shielding me. "It could still be a trap."

I touched his arm. "Let's wait. Just a moment."

The drone paused about twenty feet away, its metal casing glinting softly in the late sunlight. Then it dipped slightly, as if bowing.

A panel on its front clicked open, and a small projection blinked to life – just light, no sound at first. Then static, followed by a distorted voice.

"Hazel? Hazel Morris?"

The voice was female. And it was probably wishful thinking, but it sounded human.

"This is Fay MacLean from the *Bloodstar*. We've been searching for you. Please – if you can hear this – "

Fallin stiffened beside me. "*Bloodstar*," he murmured. "Do you know them?"

I shook my head, slowly. "No. But they clearly know me."

Another crackle.

"We've been trying to locate the last human survivor from the Trials. You're not alone anymore. The game makers have been neutralised. We're here to help."

The last human survivor. That had to mean me.

I stared at the drone, heart pounding. Was this real? Was help finally here?

The drone hovered, silent and still, like it was waiting. Not threatening – just watching.

Fallin moved a little closer to me, shielding without smothering. "It could be a trap. How can they have defeated the game makers? It's impossible."

"Or it could be the truth." My voice trembled, but I didn't care. "They knew I was out here. They knew my name."

The next crackle no longer made me shrink back. "We are about to land on Kalumbu. Venom says the coordinates should show up in just a second."

"What's a *second*?" Fallin whispered.

"More proof that she is human. In my language, it's the shortest unit of time. It's about as long as it takes to say twenty-one."

The drone's light shimmered and turned into the projection of a simple map. Two dots blinked rapidly.

Fallin pointed at the one on the left. "That's us. I recognise the mountains over there. I think I know where they are."

The probe stuttered, then the map disappeared. It remained hovering in place, blinking gently.

I turned to him. "What do we do? Fly there?"

His wings flexed once, a sharp movement of tension. "We don't trust them. Not yet."

"But maybe," I said slowly, "we listen."

His tail looped around my ankle. Protective. Uncertain.

"If this is a trick," he said, "I'll burn the sky itself."

I reached out and took his hand. "And if it's not?"

"Then we may have a future."

The flight took about half an hour. Fallin had commanded Ruby to return to the other tyvarin in order to keep her safe. She'd protested but eventually bent to his will.

The last sunlight was almost gone by the time we reached the edge of the forest. A wide river would have blocked our way if we'd been on foot, but Fallin's wings safely carried us across and to the grassland on the other side. A space shuttle was parked in the centre of the bright pink grass. So this is how crop circles were made. On its ramp, two human women were standing, shielding their eyes against the setting sun. I realised how cleverly Fallin had planned our approach, giving us an advantage. We could observe them easily, while they had to look right into the sunlight.

Fallin landed at a safe distance, steadying me as he

set me on the ground. The grass reached almost to my shoulder. Insects buzzed. Hopefully none that would bite. But knowing what this planet was like, most of them were probably deadly.

"Let's have them come to us," he said. His wings were still open, ready to jump into the air at the slightest threat. He really didn't trust them.

And maybe nor should I. What were the chances of two human women coming to our rescue? It was ridiculous. But so was me being on an alien planet in the company of a dragon shifter.

The women stepped down the ramp with caution, but no visible fear. The taller one had auburn hair and a wary, assessing gaze that reminded me of a predator watching for movement. The other was shorter, her light brown curls tied back in a messy bun. She looked exhausted but determined, her posture tense, like she was holding something fragile inside her and refused to let it crack.

Realising that we weren't going to come any closer, they made their way through the sea of pink grass.

"Any sign of trouble, we're gone," Fallin whispered, tension radiating off him in waves.

For some reason, I was less worried. These two women did not look threatening at all. And they were humans!

"Could they be... I don't know, holograms? Somehow presenting themselves as looking like humans, but they aren't actually?"

Fallin snarled softly. "With the game makers, you

never know. They excel at deception. And this would be great entertainment: we hope for allies, only to be attacked and defeated. Stay wary. I don't trust them."

When they got close enough for our voices to carry, the taller one raised her hand in a small wave. Next to me, Fallin stiffened.

"I'm Fay. This is Clare. We come in peace." To my surprise, she chuckled. "Never thought I'd ever use that sentence. I'm feeling very Star Trek just now."

I couldn't help but grin. Fallin clearly didn't get the reference, but he stayed silent.

The other woman, Clare, also gave us a wave. "We'd almost given up hope. Those dragons kept destroying the drones we sent to get in touch with you. In the end, we decided coming in person was a better option."

I realised she didn't know that Fallin was one of the dragons. Yes, he looked like a lizardman with his scales and wings, but he was nowhere near as scary as when I'd first met him as Tyvaron.

I took a deep breath. "I'm Hazel, but you seem to already know that. How do you know me? And who are you, exactly?"

Fay laughed again, a sound that reminded me of tiny bells. "It's a very long story. The short version is that both of us, along with other women, were kidnapped from Earth and brought here to take part in something called the Trials of Kalumbu. The game makers didn't expect us to survive for long, but some-how, all of us not only survived, but we met our mates and made it off the planet. As I said, it's a long story. And I see you have also met another contestant..."

I realised she wanted me to introduce Fallin.

"This is Fallin." I didn't correct her assumption that he was a contestant, nor did I give them any other information. I sensed Fallin appreciated my decision to hold back for now.

"Great to meet you," Clare said with another wave. "Anyway, after eight of us had managed to gather on a spaceship, the Bloodstar, we had to decide whether to flee or to fight the game makers. We knew there was one more woman in the Trials and others on the space station orbiting the planet, so it was an easy decision. We had help, though. The Intergalactic Authority-"

"That's the space police," Fay added.

"-they helped. To be fair, they did most of the work. Took over the space station, captured the game makers, freed the captives, including the remaining human women. It's all been quite chaotic, but Venom, my mate, realised he could use the game makers' drones to search for you. He's a hacker and... Anyway. We found you. You are safe now."

"She is already safe," Fallin growled.

Fay raised an eyebrow. "You managed to get a possessive one. Wait until he meets Vruhag. My orc."

"Orc?" I echoed, speechless. I felt like I'd been transported into a different reality. Just when I'd got used to an alien world filled with dragons and monsters, everything had shifted yet again.

"Shall we go somewhere more comfortable? The

sound of all these insects is giving me the creeps. I've spent enough time on Kalumbu to know that most things here bite. Trust me, it wasn't easy to come back."

Trust. Could I. Could we?

I exchanged a look with Fallin. He didn't look convinced, but he'd lost some of his earlier wariness.

"I won't enter your shuttle," he said finally, the first words he'd exchanged with the women. "But we can go closer to the riverbank. It's safer there."

He wrapped me in his arms and flew me the twenty metres or so to the edge of the river, where large smooth boulders offered seating opportunities. We could have walked, but I knew that this was a symbolic move. He wanted to show them that we did not trust them - yet. And that he was powerful. He could fly. He had been on this planet for much longer than all of them combined. If he wanted to, he could defeat them without breaking a sweat.

When we were all seated on rocks – Fallin stayed standing by my side, wings half-extended - Clare took a slow breath.

"I wasn't sure we'd find you," she said, voice quieter now. "This place is deadly. It's a miracle you survived for this many days. Honestly, some days I can barely believe Venom and I made it out."

She glanced at Fay, then back to me. "Venom and I were holed up in a mountain cave, hiding from the game makers' drones. We were surrounded. It was looking bad. But we had managed to contact the Bloodstar."

She hesitated, eyes flicking to Fallin. "Then the dragon came. Huge. Shimmering scales, eyes like molten gold. It attacked the cave from the outside. I thought that was it – we were done for."

Next to me, Fallin shifted his weight.

"But when we ran out to board the shuttle, he didn't attack," Clare continued. "He hesitated. Watched us. I could *feel* how strong he was – one swipe and we'd have been gone. But something made him stop. He looked right at me... and he let us live."

She smiled faintly. "That dragon saved our lives. I didn't understand it then. I still don't. But I've never forgotten it."

Fallin stepped forward slowly. "I remember," he said, voice low. "I was still under the masters' influence. Partially. But something about you..." He glanced briefly at me. "And about Venom. I saw a bond between you. It reminded me of something I'd lost."

Clare's eyes widened. "I don't understand."

Fallin squeezed my shoulder, then he stepped back into the open grass and shifted – scales, wings, light. Tyvaron emerged once more.

Clare stared up at him, awe and recognition dawning in her face. "You... It is you! You spared us."

Tyvaron dipped his head, his voice booming. "And I would again."

The breeze tugged at my wings, lifting the edges as if trying to carry me skyward once more. But I stayed grounded.

Hazel stood beside me, one hand resting on my forearm like a tether to the present. Across from us, Clare stared, her expression caught between awe and gratitude. Fay, however, looked thoughtful. Calculating.

"I still can't believe it was you," Clare said. "Back in the mountains... you could have killed us."

"I almost did," I admitted. "But something stopped me. I didn't understand it then. I do now."

Hazel's grip tightened slightly – not possessive, just... anchoring. I let the form of Tyvaron fall away, bone and scale retreating until I stood once again as Fallin. Just a male. Not a weapon. Not a monster.

Just hers.

We sat again, closer now. The river burbled softly

in the background, a quiet reminder that the world was still turning – even after everything.

"What now?" I asked, directing the question at Fay.

She didn't answer immediately. "Now that the game makers are gone, Kalumbu is... in transition. The Intergalactic Authority has taken control of the station and the orbiting satellites. They've shut down the Trials permanently. No more contestants. No more drones hunting for blood."

Hazel looked up sharply. "Are the other women... are they going back to Earth?"

Fay's smile faltered. "That's... complicated."

Clare leaned forward gently. "Hazel, I'm so sorry. We all hoped the same, at first. That once it was over, we'd go home. But..." She looked at Fay for support.

"You were in cryosleep," Fay said softly. "We all were. For a long time."

Hazel frowned. "How long?"

I sensed the answer before they spoke. I pulled Hazel closer, cradled her in my arms, showing her that I was here for her, no matter what. No matter what Fay was about to say.

"Seventy years."

Silence.

Hazel didn't move. Didn't speak. Just blinked.

"Earth's changed," Clare added. "We don't know what's waiting there now. Most of us don't have anyone left. Even if we did, they're old, or gone. And there are other complications... the IA's still assessing whether it's even safe or ethical to repatriate humans from the

Trials. For now, we've been offered a special refugee citizenship that gives us the right to stay here or move to wherever we want."

Hazel nodded slowly. "Right. So there's no home to go back to."

Her voice didn't shake – but her fingers curled into mine.

"You have a home with me," I said. Not to comfort her. Not to claim her. Just to say the truth.

Her smile was small. But it was real.

"I need to talk to the other tyvarin," I said, shifting the focus. "Some of them may want to stay. Make Kalumbu into something new – a haven instead of a prison. We were preparing for war. Now we can prepare for peace."

"And you?" Fay asked.

I met her gaze. "I want to go home. To *my* world. I don't even know if it still exists, but I have to try. I remember pieces now – names, places, skies. I want to find my people. If there are any left."

"You'll need a ship," Fay said. "I'm sure the IA can arrange something. They owe us more than a ride."

Hazel turned to me. "Will you take me with you?"

I raised her hand to my lips. "I would never leave without you. And if you prefer to stay here, with these females, then so be it."

Fay smiled again, this time warmer. "We'll talk to the others. I'm sure something can be arranged."

"We'll need more than that," I said. "If Kalumbu is

to become a sanctuary for the tyvarin who stay, we'll need supplies. Protection."

"The IA will help," Clare said. "They've already started rebuilding the station. It's not much, but it's a start."

A start. It was more than we'd had before.

Fay rose first. "We should let you rest and discuss everything. You've both been through... far more than most."

Clare pulled a small device from her jacket and handed it to Hazel. "This is a comm beacon. Standard IA issue. If you need us or want to talk, press the top pad. We'll get your signal – even from orbit."

Hazel turned it over in her hands. "Thank you."

Clare offered a soft smile. "We'll have people in the area for a few more days while the IA finishes clearing the last of the game maker tech. They don't want anyone to come and restart the Trials. They're also discussing moving the beasts that were brought to Kalumbu. Some have made this their home, but their species aren't endemic to this planet. Take your time to talk through your options. There is no time limit on anything the IA offers." She turned to me. "And don't worry. We won't come uninvited."

"Tell your friends," I said quietly. "That this land belongs to the tyvarin now. We will defend it. And that the lab we were created in is out of bounds. We need access to the tech in there."

Fay gave a sharp nod. "I'll make sure they understand that. The IA wants peace – and frankly, after what they found on the station, they want distance too."

Clare touched Hazel's arm. "It really is over. You're safe."

Hazel smiled faintly. "I hope you're right."

Then they turned, crossed the pink grass, and disappeared into the shuttle. A moment later, the vessel's thrusters hummed to life. I wrapped Hazel in my arms as the shuttle lifted and ascended into the orange sky, streaking upward until it vanished into the upper atmosphere.

Silence settled again.

Except this time, it wasn't tense. Just still.

We sat together by the river's edge. Hazel's knees were drawn to her chest, the comm beacon resting on a smooth rock beside her. I kept my tail looped gently around her legs – not tight, just there. A touch of grounding.

"Seventy years," she said at last. "I didn't even think I'd been asleep. My body feels the same. The only sign that something had happened was my shortened hair. But... everyone I knew... they're gone."

I didn't speak. I knew nothing I could say would change that. But I stayed close. And I listened.

"I was twenty-eight on the last day I remember spending on Earth. It was just an ordinary day. Work. I got a takeaway on the way home. Fish and chips with extra salt and vinegar. Do they even still have fish and chips on Earth? What if world war three happened? What if Scotland got nuked? What if humanity is extinct?"

She laughed once – bitter and lightless.

"I should feel grief. But I don't think I've even begun to process it."

I reached over and brushed a strand of hair from her face. "There is no right way to grieve time that was stolen. You don't owe anyone a certain reaction."

She looked at me then. "Would you go back? If your planet's still out there?"

"Yes," I said without hesitation. "Not to escape this place – but to remember who I was before they took it from me. I need to know if my clan still lives. If Vareth-kai still floats above the clouds. If my name means anything there."

She nodded slowly. "And I would come with you?"

I tilted her chin so she'd look me in the eyes. "Hazel, if you don't want to follow me to Valhyr's Crown – then I'll change course. I'll build us a home here, in the mountains, or in the forest. You are my future. My home."

Her smile trembled at the edges, but it was genuine. "Let's find your world," she said. "If it's gone, we'll make a new one. Together."

She took a deep breath and exhaled, letting go of something she'd been holding onto until now.

"Should we get back? The tyvarin will be wondering where we are."

I wanted to stay here a little longer, give her more

time to talk about her grief, but she was right. I'd left the tyvarin without telling them where we were going. They'd be worried. And in their fragile state of re-awakening, that was not a good thing.

We took flight just after moonrise. Hazel curled against my chest, the wind flattening her hair against her face as we rose towards the mountains again. The forest below was a sea of black and silver. The fires of the tyvarin camp were visible even from this distance – faint orange glows scattered like stars fallen to earth.

As we flew, I thought of the others.

How many would want to leave?

How many would fear what waited beyond Kalumbu?

And how many would choose – for the first time in their lives – to build something all their own?

We would give them the choice.

And this time, no one would take it from them.

The wind bit a little harder at this altitude. Colder. Sharper. Or maybe it was just my nerves.

The glow of the signal fires came into view first, flickering steadily like eyes in the dark. There were more of them now – at least twice as many as when we'd left. That meant more dragons had arrived. More minds to reach. More hearts to convince.

Fallin circled the plateau once before descending, wings taut with tension. I could feel it in his body, the way his muscles clenched beneath my palms. He wasn't scared, but he wasn't at ease either.

We landed at the edge of the clearing, where the stone was cracked and veined with pale moss. Ruby greeted us with wild chirps and happy flaps of her wings. No one else stepped forward to greet us.

But they were watching. Waiting.

Shapes moved in the shadows – hulking bodies,

wings tucked close, eyes glowing in the gloom. I saw scars. Mismatched horns. Tails coiled like questions. Some still bore their collars like broken shackles. Others had shed them, their necks bare, proud. Yet others were in their newly recovered forms, small among the huge dragons yet still hulking above me.

I approached the waiting tyvarin.

Fallin didn't stop me, but he stayed close – close enough that I felt his breath against my shoulder, warm and steady.

One of the larger tyvarin – a broad-chested male with a burn down one flank – stepped forward. I remembered cleaning his wounds the day before.

"You left," he said simply. His voice was deep, rough like a landslide.

"We had to meet someone," I replied. "And bring back news."

"What news?" someone else growled. I couldn't see them clearly, but I felt the ripple of distrust in the air. Like a storm about to break.

Leaving without saying anything had been a mistake. I had been so selfish, asking Fallin to come with me. I'd needed some time away, but he could have stayed, looking after his flock – what did you call a group of dragons?

Fallin moved to stand beside me, his wings flaring just enough to catch the firelight. "The game makers are gone," he said clearly. "Captured by the Intergalactic Authority. Those of you who remember their previous lives will know about them. They are the good guys. The station is no longer under the masters' control. You are safe. We are safe."

A ripple of movement passed through the crowd – a low murmur of disbelief. Smoke rose from the nostrils of one of the closest dragons.

"Their eyes still watch us," another said, his voice a hiss. "Their drones still fly."

"Remnants," Fallin replied. "Like ash after a fire. But the flame is out. The drones are now under control of the people who took over the space station. They were looking for my mate – but they will disappear now that they have fulfilled their mission. We're free – truly free now. And we have a choice."

"You sound like them," someone muttered. "Talking about freedom like it's a gift. Like it's not just another trap. They always promise something. They always lie."

I stepped forward again. "It's not a trap. We've seen the proof. There's a ship above us – human women who survived, just like me. They're alive. They're safe. And they offered help. Real help. Transport. Resources. The choice to stay here or to leave."

Silence.

Then the large tyvarin spoke again. "And what do you choose, Fallin of Clan Varrna?"

Fallin's jaw tightened. "I choose to return to my world. I choose to see the sky I was born under – together with my mate. But I will not leave anyone behind who doesn't want to go. If you wish to stay, to make this your home, you will not be alone. The IA will honour your safety. They've seen what we suffered. They understand."

A beat passed.

Two beats.

Then the scarred tyvarin looked at the others. "If we're truly free... then we decide together."

One by one, they stepped forward – not towards us, but towards the fires. Gathering in circles. Talking. Not shouting. Not posturing. Just... talking.

And that, more than anything, felt like victory.

Fallin let out a slow breath beside me. "They'll come around."

"They already are," I whispered. "Shall we grab some food while they're talking? I'm starving."

The tension didn't vanish, but it softened. Fallin led me to one of the smaller fires where a few of the changed tyvarin were resting. Not asleep – no one seemed ready for that – but quiet, alert, as if waiting to see which way the wind would shift.

Someone had roasted meat on a spit, and though I didn't want to think about what kind of creature it had been, the scent made my stomach growl. I hadn't realised how hungry I was. Fallin tore a strip off and handed it to me before taking a piece for himself. We sat on a smooth rock, the warmth of the fire chasing away the mountain chill.

A female tyvarin approached us. She was tall and

lithe, her scales a pale bronze that shimmered faintly in the firelight. Her wings were smaller than Fallin's, but her stance was confident – relaxed but not passive. She had the calm energy of someone who remembered who she'd once been.

"I hoped you would return," she said, her voice smoother than most of the others. "The others were close to dividing."

Fallin inclined his head. "They still might."

"I know." She glanced at me, and to my surprise, she smiled. "You're the female. The one he flies with."

I smiled back. "Hazel."

"Saavrra," she replied. "I remember that name now. It's mine."

She sat across from us, folding her legs neatly under her. "This place... it's not much. But it could be. For those who don't remember where they came from – or don't want to – it's something. Solid ground. A place to begin. I remember my past, but I do not remember it fondly. I always wanted a new beginning. Now I am offered one."

Fallin nodded slowly. "You want to stay?"

"I think I do," she said. "I think many will. Not because they're afraid. But because they want to shape something with their own claws."

I chewed my meat in silence for a moment. "And the others?"

"They'll go with you. Back to the stars. To find their kin, their homeworlds. Maybe even fight. Some will find it hard to forget the creatures they were.

Machines built for war. It is those we have to worry about."

Saavrra stood again. "They'll speak soon."

She walked away, her tail trailing through the ash.

I turned to Fallin. "Do you think it's enough? That they'll be safe here?"

He looked into the flames. "It won't be perfect. But if the IA holds to their promise, this planet can become a sanctuary."

I rested my head against his shoulder. "And for the ones who come with us? How many are there from your planet?"

"I am not sure. Saavrra is, but she does not seem like she wants to return home. There are at least four others, but there may be more. Some have changed beyond recognition."

Voices rose across the clearing. More dragons approached. A rough semi-circle was forming near the central fire. Now that they were illuminated by the flickering light, I was amazed at just how many dragons had arrived today. The group had almost doubled since this morning.

So many lives forever changed by the game makers. So many souls now desperate to reclaim their future.

One older female's voice rang out clear: "We've spoken. Some of us will remain. To build. To breathe. To finally choose our own purpose."

Another voice – one of the green-scaled males who'd shifted early – added: "The rest will go. Some with Fallin, some to other planets. To see the stars again. To find the worlds we lost."

Fallin stood. I rose with him.

The decision had been made.

And for the first time since waking up on this alien planet, I felt something more than just survival.

I felt hope.

Valhyr's Crown welcomed us home with skies of sapphire and clouds that stretched like pale silk across the horizon. Below us, jagged cliffs rose from forests of silver-barked trees and red-sheened moss. The wind here smelled as familiar as the land looked.

The outpost loomed ahead, a fair distance from the spaceport – a cluster of towers built into a mountainside, old and weathered, yet still inhabited. It had once been a gathering place for scouts and storytellers. Now it served as a waypoint for returners like us. For the draquari.

My people.

The last few weeks had passed in a blur of stars and motion. After saying goodbye to the other tyvarin – many of whom chose to remain on Kalumbu and begin new lives there – Hazel and I had boarded a slow-travel freighter heading toward this sector. Ruby had decided to come with us. The Bloodstar crew along with the IA had helped arrange everything. They'd even left us with credits and a comm device, in case we ever wished to reach out again.

We hadn't needed it. Not yet.

The human females – or Peritans, as it turned out they were known in Intergalactic Standard – had offered to meet with Hazel again, introduce her to their mates, exchange stories, but she had refused. She wanted a new start. She didn't want to hang on to the past – and that included making connections with the other females who'd shared her fate.

I supported her decision. Hopefully, she would make friends among my people. My family. I couldn't wait to introduce her to my clan.

We'd spent the voyage in a tiny private cabin, barely large enough for my wings to stretch fully, but we'd made it ours. Hazel had strung bits of yarn from the ceiling like constellations. She'd bartered for hooks and thread at every space station we stopped at, somehow always returning with a new skein of strange, colourful fibre that she insisted could be crocheted. And it could.

She made a scarf first. Then a tiny dragon plushie for Ruby, who missed the wide skies of Kalumbu. I didn't understand the appeal of yarn at first, but now I'd grown fond of the quiet clicking sound of her work, the way it soothed her. The way it soothed me.

We made love in silence and in laughter, with the stars watching through the porthole. We explored forgotten spaceports, browsed through second-hand datapads, ate food that neither of us could pronounce. It was a slow journey, but a meaningful one. Every night ended with her body curled against mine, soft and trusting, the way it was always meant to be.

Now, the end of the journey lay before us.

Or perhaps, the beginning.

Hazel stood beside me at the edge of the landing platform. Ruby circled above, spiralling with joy. Below us, in the open courtyards of the outpost, draquari moved with the ease of those who belonged. Wings shimmered in every colour imaginable – bronze, obsidian, pale opal green. They carried woven bags, metal tools, and scrolls. In this part of the planet, they held on to old traditions, forsaking technology for the simpler life. I caught a burst of song from somewhere – no words, just the long, open tones of home.

Hazel's hand found mine.

They're beautiful," she whispered. "All of them. I've never seen so many dragons before."

"*Draquari*," I said softly. "That's what we call ourselves. Dragon is... close. But not quite the same."

Her gaze flicked to me. "And you're one of them. But different."

I nodded. "The changes the masters made – they marked me."

I pushed back the edges of my tunic, revealing the seams of metal that still lined parts of my ribs. Where wings met shoulder. The iridescent shimmer across my scales, subtly different than those of the others.

Maybe one day, I could have the metal removed.

Not my inner fire, though. I had grown used to it. I'd never forgive the game makers for what they'd done to me, how they had *changed* me against my will, but I had come to the conclusion that I would use their modifications for the better. For my future.

"They used tech and trauma to make me something else. A hybrid of draquari and machine. Tyvaron, they called me – not my name, but a designation. A weapon. They did not think us worthy of names."

Hazel's fingers traced the metal, slow and reverent. "But you're still you. You're Fallin."

"I don't know how they will receive me. If the draquari will accept the man I have become." I chuckled softly. "Shall we see how they'll react to seeing Tyvaron?"

She looked at the draquari down below, going about their business, oblivious to our arrival.

"Let's do it."

I stepped back, lifting my arms to the sun. The change came effortlessly now – a cascade of heat and energy, light and memory. Wings burst free. My tail uncoiled. My claws curled into the stone beneath me.

I was myself again. I looked like Tyvaron, the leader of the tyvarin, but inside, I was Fallin of Clan Varrna. Draquari-born. Reforged.

Hazel smiled up at me, her hair caught in the wind like a living flame. She climbed onto my back with the ease of practice and settled just behind my neck, gripping the harness we'd fashioned during our journey.

Our baggage would stay here until we'd found a place to settle.

Ruby squealed with delight and swooped alongside us.

I leapt.

Wings caught the wind, muscles surged, and we soared.

Below, the world stretched vast and untouched. Rivers wove through valleys like liquid silver. Canyons split the land like old scars. And far ahead – the mountains. Tall, proud, eternal.

My homeland.

Hazel whooped behind me, the sound carried away on the wind. I could feel her joy – her awe – and it filled my chest until I thought I would burst with it.

Beneath us, draquari looked up in surprise, some in fear. A few spread their wings and leapt into the air, either out of instinct or recognition. I didn't know which.

We flew past them – not fleeing, not attacking, simply gliding in wide, regal arcs over their heads. My wings cast long shadows over the courtyards and towers below. I angled toward the far cliffs, where the wind curled strong and wild. Where the old paths carved into stone still marked the way to Vareth-kai.

Home.

The ridges were steeper here, red rock veined with glinting silver ore, cliffs draped in climbing vines that shimmered with dew. As we neared, I saw it – the plateau where my family's hearth had once burned. It was still there. Cracked and weathered, yes. Overgrown. But not destroyed.

Hazel leaned close. "Is this it?"

"Yes," I said, voice deep with memory. "This is where I was born. Where I took my first flight. Where my father taught me to catch the wind, and my mother sang the names of the stars."

I landed with care, not wanting to disturb the sacred ground. Hazel slid from my back, touching down lightly, reverently. Ruby landed beside us, flapping her tiny wings and chirping like she knew this place mattered.

I shifted back to my smaller form, kneeling to press my palm into the warm stone. For a moment, I didn't speak. I just breathed. Let the past settle into my bones.

"I remember chasing shadows here," I said finally. "My brothers and I carved our names into that wall." I gestured to a craggy outcrop now half-covered in moss. "We made promises here. Swore we'd never be parted. That nothing could break us."

Hazel knelt beside me, her hand finding mine. "Do you think they're still out there?"

"I don't know." My throat tightened. "But I'll find out."

She squeezed my fingers. "Then this is where we begin."

A cry echoed in the distance – not a roar of alarm, but a call. A signal. Draquari approaching, wings beating the wind in slow, curious rhythm.

"They're coming," I murmured.

Hazel stood, brushing her hair from her face. "Should I hide?"

"No." I looked up at her, heart full. "You stand beside me. You are my mate. My strength. My future."

She nodded, quiet and sure. "Then let them come."

And so we waited, the wind around us full of song, of memories, of new beginnings.

I rose slowly to my feet, Hazel at my side, as two draquari descended in a wide arc and landed a respectful distance away. One was younger, unfamiliar. The other – older, broad-shouldered, his wings tinged with iron-grey, one of his horns broken at the tip, and his brow marked with the tattoos of clan leadership.

Recognition hit me like a bolt of lightning.

"Vekorr?" I said, breath catching.

He blinked, then stepped forward slowly, as if not daring to believe. "Fallin?"

I nodded once. "It's me."

A shudder passed through him – then he crossed the distance in a few long strides and seized me in a crushing embrace. His strength hadn't faded in the years I'd been gone. His arms locked around me like he was anchoring me to the world.

"We thought you were dead," he rasped. "We searched every sector. We sent messages across systems. Your brothers went mad with grief. Your mother... gods, Fallin. She still sets a place for you."

I swallowed hard, barely able to breathe. Hazel stood just behind me, silent but present, her hand warm at my back.

"They took me," I said. "Pirates. They brought me to Kalumbu. Have you heard of the Trials? The game makers there turned me into a weapon and erased my name. But I broke free. I remembered. I came home."

Vekorr stepped back, eyes scanning me – the metal at my sides, the shimmer of altered scale, the fire that still lived in my eyes. But he did not flinch. He simply nodded. "You are still of Clan Varrna. And you are whole enough to return. That is all that matters."

Then he turned his gaze to Hazel, curious but not unfriendly.

"Who is the one who brought you back?"

I nodded, and Hazel gave a tentative smile. "Hazel. I'm... not from here."

"She is my mate," I explained. "The stars led her to me."

Vekorr looked at me again, then smiled at us both. "Then she is one of us now. You both are."

My throat closed. I'd imagined my return a thousand different ways. Not one of them included being welcomed home by the clan elder, my uncle.

He turned to the other draquari and murmured a short message in our old tongue – a call of welcome, of return, of gathering. Then he looked back at us, his eyes glinting.

"Come. The fires are still lit at the hall. The hearth never went out. Your family will want to see you. And the stars will want your stories."

Hazel looked up at me, eyes wide and shining.

I squeezed her hand.

"Let's go home," I said.

---

*This is the end of Hazel and Fallin's story – almost.
Read an exclusive bonus scene here:*
skyemackinnon.com/dragon-bonus

*Discover the world of the Starlight Monsters by starting
the series with* My Big Sweet Waffle Monster.

*This is only one of many series set in the Starlight
Universe. How about some alien Highlanders (Starlight
Highlanders),* Vikings (Starlight Vikings), *Pirates
(Alien Abduction for Pirates) or alien reverse harem
(The Intergalactic Guide to Humans, Vol. 1)?*

*For all the latest releases, author updates and cat
pictures, subscribe to my newsletter:*
skyemackinnon.com/newsletter

THE STARLIGHT UNIVERSE

This book is part of the Starlight Universe, an entire galaxy filled with hunky aliens, exotic planets, and the human women ready to find love among the stars.

Starlight Highlanders Mail Order Brides

Alien Highlanders in kilts come to Earth in search of brides... and take them to planet Albya. Three m/f standalones full of humour, action and steamy romance. Part of the Intergalactic Dating Agency.

Starlight Vikings

Set on Earth and on the spaceship Valkyr, this trilogy of m/f standalones is all about hunky alien Vikings in need of females. Part of the Intergalactic Dating Agency.

Starlight Mermen

Hundreds of years ago, they crash-landed on Earth

and gave rise to many of our legends. Now, they're back, desperate for female mates. Part of the Intergalactic Dating Agency.

The Intergalactic Guide to Humans

A humorous take on alien abductions, probing and other shenanigans. One reverse harem trilogy about clueless aliens and the human woman they abducted, followed by several standalone romances with various pairings (m/f, f/m/f and m/m). If you want light entertainment filled with unicorns, fabulous misunderstandings and unusual body parts, this is the series for you.

Starlight Monsters

These aliens are not your usual humanoids... they have claws, fangs, tails, scales, knotty dicks and will growl at you. Interconnected m/f standalones with lots of action, steam and fated mates.

ABOUT THE AUTHOR

Skye MacKinnon is a Scottish romance author who was raised by elves in the mystical Highlands and calls the Loch Ness monster her friend. Her bestselling books weave together romance with action, suspense and whimsical humour, creating page-turners filled with strong heroines, alpha heroes and loveable monsters.

Whether she's writing about aliens in kilts, hunky Vikings or cat shifter assassins, Skye likes to put a new spin on familiar tropes. Some of her heroines don't have to choose, some fall in love with other women, and others get abducted by clueless aliens.

Skye lives with her bossy cat on the west coast of Scotland and uses the dramatic views from her office as an inspiration, no matter whether she writes fantasy, paranormal or science fiction romance. Until she gets abducted by aliens, that is.

Subscribe to her newsletter:
skyemackinnon.com/newsletter

Buy your books direct from the author

GET 20% OFF YOUR NEXT
EBOOK OR AUDIOBOOK!

USE CODE BOOKWORMS AT
SKYEMACKINNON.COM/SHOP

EBOOKS, AUDIOBOOKS, PRINT BOOKS,
MERCHANDISE & MORE

Find all of Skye's books on her website, **skyemackinnon.com**, where you can also order signed paperbacks and swag.

Many of her books are available as audiobooks.

SCIENCE FICTION ROMANCE

Set in the Starlight Universe

- **Starlight Vikings** (sci-fi m/f romance)
- **Starlight Mermen** (sci-fi m/f romance)
- **Starlight Monsters** (sci-fi m/f romance)
- **Starlight Highlanders Mail Order Brides** (sci-fi m/f romance)
- **The Intergalactic Guide to Humans** (sci-fi romance with various pairings)

Set in other worlds

- **Between Rebels** (sci-fi reverse harem set in the Planet Athion shared world)
- **The Mars Diaries** (sci-fi reverse harem)
- **Aliens and Animals** (f/f sci-fi romance co-written with Arizona Tape)

PARANORMAL & FANTASY ROMANCE

- **Claiming Her Bears** (post-apocalyptic shifter reverse harem)
- **Daughter of Winter** (fantasy reverse harem)
- **Catnip Assassins** (urban fantasy reverse harem)
- **Infernal Descent** (paranormal reverse harem based on Dante's Inferno, co-written with Bea Paige)
- **Seven Wardens** (fantasy reverse harem co-written with Laura Greenwood)
- **The Lost Siren** (post-apocalyptic, paranormal reverse harem co-written with Liza Street)

OTHER SERIES

- **Academy of Time** (time travel academy standalones, reverse harem and m/f)
- **Defiance** (contemporary reverse harem with a hint of thriller/suspense)

STANDALONES

- Song of Souls – m/f fantasy romance, fairy tale retelling
- Highland Butterflies – sapphic romance
- Wings of Time and Fate - epic fantasy

BOX SETS

- Daggers & Destiny – a fantasy romance starter library
- Stars & Seduction - a science fiction romance starter library